THE UNIVERSE IN which Castle Falkenstein, King Ludwig's lavish fortress, was reality rather than royal daydream was a rich, red-velvet Victorian. Nothing like alien space beings had ever cropped up in it, nor were they likely to. They just didn't belong here, and Tom couldn't believe Moriarty's conspiracy theories. Other universes, Tom had been assured by faerie folk who knew, were very high-tech, and featured ray guns, interstellar travel, and other wonders. But not old Falkenstein, the universe of sabers, steam tech, and pepperbox pistols. True, in the Falkenstein universe the nineteenth century always threatened to become the twentieth ahead of schedule, if certain other nasty faerie folk, namely the Unsee~~lie had their way. But~~ Tom's mission w~~as~~ twentieth centur~~y~~ ond before it abs~~orbed~~

Other Proteus Fantasy Novels
Now Available from Prima!

How to Order:

For information on quantity discounts contact the publisher: Prima Publishing, P.O. Box 1260BK, Rocklin, CA 95677-1260; (916) 632-4400. On your letterhead include information concerning the intended use of the books and the number of books you wish to purchase. For individual orders, turn to the back of the book for more information.

Masterminds of Falkenstein

A Castle Falkenstein™ Novel

by
John DeChancie

PRIMA PUBLISHING

ISBN: 0-7615-0484-2
Library of Congress Catalog Card Number: 96-067863
Printed in the United States of America
96 97 98 99 EE 10 9 8 7 6 5 4 3 2 1

To Mike Pondsmith, the Creator.

Preface:
What Has Gone Before

OVER UNCOUNTABLE MILLENNIA, a bitter state of war has existed between two rival factions of the *faerie*, a powerful race of energy creatures that exist in a nebulous other universe called the *Faerie Veil*.

Championed by the enigmatic Lord Auberon, the Seelie Court of Faerie works to defend humanity everywhere from the gibbering hordes of their mortal enemies, the Unseelie. Led by the Adversary, Auberon's arch-enemy, the utterly horrific Unseelie want nothing less than to *eat* humanity, body and soul.

In the alternate steampunk world of New Europa, both sides have reached a stalemate in a sorcerous cold war. The Adversary manipulates the forces of ambitious human Chancellor Otto von Bismarck and his new Prussian Empire; Lord Auberon leads a small band of human and faerie freedom fighters determined to undo the Unseelie's evil plans.

The Adversary schemes to eliminate the young King Ludwig II of the peaceful kingdom of Bavaria (Bayern, in the Faerie Veil), paving the way for the Prussian's total conquest of all New Europa. The wily Auberon enlists the aid of his human friend, Grey Morrolan, Illuminatus Mage, and manages to save Ludwig—but only for the moment. Knowing time is running out, the two invoke their magic to reach through the multiverse for a champion who can turn the tide against the forces of darkness.

What they *get* is Tom Olam, a computer game artist spellnapped from our own twentieth century. However unwittingly, Tom bears the salvation of New Europa—a copy of the lost *Principia Magica* of Leonardo da Vinci. A harmless sketchbook in our world, in New Europa this tome becomes a powerful *Grimoire* that details the creation of Magickal Engines—sorcerous devices that cast spells.

Rhyme Enginemaster, Ludwig's cranky but brilliant handyman, sets to work deciphering the secrets of Leonardo's book. He combines magick with his own Dwarfen talents to launch a fleet of Aerial Battleships against a Prussian invasion of Bayern.

The forces clash in the titanic battle of Königseig, where Ludwig's rag-tag skyfleet bombs the Land-

Fortresses off the field and victory falls to the Bayernese. Secure on his throne, Ludwig and his allies
thwart Bismarck's ambitions to unite the German
states under Prussian rule. The peaceful nations of
the world unite with the Seelie Court and sign the
Second Compact. This revolutionary agreement com-
mits man and faerie to fight the Unseelie wherever
they manifest, in an effort to stave off a coming revolution of steam and steel and the dark future that
Tom Olam knows only too well . . .

Tom, who was instrumental in the victory at
Königseig, becomes one of King Ludwig's most trusted secret agents. He travels the world, often in the
company of the beautiful and deadly Countess Marianne, thwarting evil wherever it arises. Among their
exploits:

• Notorious evil mastermind Fu Manchu kidnaps
not only a young Sherlock Holmes, but Countess
Marianne as well. A deadly transcontinental race
ensues as Tom, accompanied by mathematics stu-
dent James Moriarty, tracks the evil Sai Fan Master to his hidden fortress beneath the Forbidden
City of Peking. (The forthcoming novel *A League of
Dragons* by G.A. Effinger (Prima Publishing) details
this adventure.)

• The Bayernese Secret Service discovers that the
Prussians are working on a new super-weapon—
guided intercontinental rockets! With visions of Nazi

V-weapons flashing through his head, Tom travels across New Europa in search of the people and knowledge that will help him thwart Bismarck. Among the allies he enlists is the mysterious Captain Nemo. He also encounters his erstwhile ally Moriarty, now the evil head of the World Crime League—in the sewers of Paris, no less! (*From Prussia with Love*, by noted fantasy author John DeChancie—author of the book you're reading now—and also available from Prima Publishing, chronicles that epic.)

• In 1876 comes one of Tom's most exciting adventures. Following the clues in a nightmare, Tom travels to America. There he discovers the dark machinations of the Freemasons of the United States, battles plague in the Voudon-haunted streets of New Orleans, and goes to a barbecue with the Indian Twenty Nations Confederation. He learns the meaning of the nightmare and secures another alliance before journeying on to San Francisco, capital of the Bear Flag Empire of California.

There he meets the mad Norton I, Emperor of California and Protector of Mexico. Tom discerns the method in Norton's madness, though, and cements a new alliance between the Empire and Bayern. (The role-playing games of R. Talsorian Games, Inc. Of Berkeley, California set up this and many other fantasy adventures.)

In this world beyond the Faerie Veil, challenges never cease. Adventures send Tom and Marianne to the ends of the Earth; now, for example, they must return to America, and to a new and dastardly threat confronting their friends in the Bear Flag Empire.

One

T HIS WAY, SIRS," the bellhop said, turning to the right as he stepped off the elevator.

"What's your name again, fella?"

"Jarvis, sir." Jarvis was a young man with curly red hair.

"You from San Francisco?"

"Yes, sir."

"I'm from the States. Brooklyn. You sure you don't originally come from the States?"

"No, sir, like I said, I was born right here in the Bear Flag Empire."

"Yeah? I live in Paris now. So does Jean-Claude, here."

"Must be great, sir, living in Paris."

"It's a living."

"You gentlemen here for the World Science Convention?"

"Yeah, that's it."

"Here's your room, sir."

Jarvis set down the heavy suitcases and twisted the key in the lock. Opening the door, he waited for the two guests—both tall and beefy and kind of rough around the edges, not your usual scientist types—to pass through. He then followed with the suitcases.

It was one of the hotel's nicest suites, a full apartment with two bedrooms, a sitting room, two baths with fancy fixtures, and a small kitchen and dining area, complete with a dining table featuring an elaborate floral centerpiece.

"You the only fellows staying here?" Jarvis asked.

"Why?" Jean-Claude wanted to know, suddenly suspicious.

"Just asking, sir."

"We're waiting for a colleague to arrive," the friendly one said mildly.

Jean-Claude grabbed Jarvis by both lapels. "You recognize me, eh? My face, you've seen it?"

"Take it easy, sir. I've never seen you before in my life."

"Jean-Claude, come on," the other one said. "We're all the way across the world, for crissake."

"He knows us, Jim." Jean-Claude pronounced it "Jeem."

Jim said, "You don't know us, do you, kid?"

"No, sir! Like I said, never laid eyes on you."

"I don't like bellboy asking so many questions."

"I didn't ask so many questions, sir. Really, I didn't."

"Let him go, Jean-Claude."

"I don't like him. He is maybe Pinkerton."

"I'm no Pink," Jarvis protested.

"Don't be so nosy." With one meaty hand, Jean-Claude took hold of Jarvis's nose between thumb and forefinger and gave it a vicious tweak.

Jarvis yelped and jumped back, holding his nose. Eyes tearing, he held it until it stopped throbbing. Then, without preamble, while Jean-Claude was turned to his pal, both having a good laugh, he drove his fist into Jean-Claude's middle. Following up with a right cross to the face, he stepped back to watch Jean-Claude go crashing into the dining table. The table cracked in two, bringing the silver service, the finger bowls, the serviettes, the floral centerpiece, and the gilded candlesticks down on him. When the crashing and tumbling stopped, Jean-Claude picked himself slowly up from the expensive debris.

Jim grunted. "You can use your fists, fella." Then he reached into his waistcoat and took out a small revolver. "A little too good for a bellhop."

"Hey, now," Jarvis said, backing away.

"OK, talk, copper—or whatever you are."

"Nothing to talk about."

"I kill him," Jean-Claude said, taking out his revolver. He took aim.

Jim yelled, "Wait!"

Jarvis turned and made a dash for the door. The revolver barked, and Jarvis slammed against the wall and fell. Although badly wounded, he managed to get to his feet and fall out the door before the gun fired again. The second shot missed him, but the first had done its work.

Staggering down the hall, Jarvis Gresham resolved not to go back to the room and open windows to air the place out, or to hang up suits.

Some guests just didn't deserve special treatment.

THE CLERK AT the desk of the Palace Hotel, a Mr. Hingham, tapped the bell that summoned bellhops, but none appeared immediately, which peeved Hingham to no end. This was the Palace, the most prestigious hotel in the city of San Francisco, and it more than prided itself on service; in fact, the Palace, although built very recently, was universally regarded as the poshest hotel in town, catering to a select clientele.

The lobby was pure splendor: an open court rising six levels, roofed by an immense skylight. The court was big enough to have a turnaround for a constant stream of carriages, from which alighted the great and near-great of the world. On the West Coast of the continent, the Palace Hotel set the standard for luxury. All the world agreed, and all the world came to the Palace. It was truly an international hotel—or at least it was trying hard to be. San Francisco, capital of the "Bear Flag Empire" of California, was also the gateway to the Orient.

"I must apologize," Mr. Hingham said to the distinguished guest waiting in front of the desk. "Usually bellhops shoot out of the bell captain's station the moment I ring. But we've just had a change of management, and things haven't been normal since. I do hope you forgive this inconvenience, Dr. Verne. *Pardonnez-nous, s'il vous plaît.*"

"Ah, you speak French," said Jules Verne.

"Un peu," Hingham said self-deprecatingly. *"C'est negligeable."*

"On the contrary, you speak fine. I do not do as well with English. My books are printed here in translation, but I cannot read them. Not well, anyway. Ah, here is . . . how do you say? The bellboy. In France, they are called—"

"Mr. Jarvis, may I say that you are inexcusably sluggish this afternoon."

Jarvis Gresham hobbled up to the desk and stood slumped over, gripping the travertine desktop, knuckles white.

"Yes, Mr. Hingham."

Hingham did a double take. "See here, young man. What in the world is wrong with you? Are you ill? Why are you holding your side like that?"

Jarvis swallowed. "Mr. Hingham, I must speak to one of the guests. A Mr. North, in Room . . ."

"What? You'll do no such thing. Besides, he hasn't checked in yet. Why on earth—never mind. Wait till I check this gentleman in, and you can—Jarvis! What is it?"

Jarvis Gresham fell face forward onto the marble floor of the lobby.

Verne squatted and examined the young man lying at his feet. *"Mon Dieu,* this man has been shot!"

"What!" Mr. Hingham's face drained. "Oh, dear. This can't happen!"

"What happened?" came a voice behind Verne.

Verne looked up and saw a lean, handsome, mustachioed American in a suit with a Western cut. He wore cowboy boots of lavishly hand-tooled leather, buffed to a sheen. Something about the outfit said "Texas," unmistakably.

"This man has been shot," Verne said. "I think he is dead. No, not quite. He is trying to say something."

The Texan got to his knees and bent over to listen. Verne listened, too.

"Auto . . . ma . . ."

"Eh? What is that?" Verne urged. "Again?"

"Auto . . . auto . . . ma . . ."

"I think he is saying 'automotive,'" Verne ventured. The Texan shook his head. "I can't make it out."

Jarvis said no more. Verne took his pulse. Presently, the Frenchman rose.

"This man is dead."

A stir had commenced in the lobby, and curious people began to gather round. Verne and the Texan did their best to keep the crowd from closing in.

"Where's the house dick?" the Texan demanded.

"My dear sir," Hingham said. "'Detective,' please. And you are . . . ?"

"Hollister. Jake Hollister. OK, 'detective,' but where is he?"

"I am the house detective," said a gravelly voice to Hollister's right. Hollister rose to confront a tall, stone-faced man in a black suit. His face was almost expressionless, his skin curiously waxen and sallow.

"I will take over from here. You, you . . ." The man jabbed a finger at the other bellboys, who were standing around in a daze. "Pick him up, carry him to my office. Quick."

"What's your name, sir?" Hollister said.

The detective fixed Hollister with intense black eyes. "Quintus is the name."

"Quintus," Hollister said, nodding. "You'll inform the police?"

"Of course I will inform the police. Do not attempt to tell me my job, Mr. . . ."

"Hollister. Jacob Hollister, Fort Worth. I wouldn't presume."

Quintus's thin lips turned upward into an approximation of a smile. "Mr. Hollister, I must apologize for this inconvenience. Good day, and have a pleasant stay in our hotel."

Verne and the American stepped back and let the detective take over. No fewer than five bellboys picked up the body and carried it off. The crowd dispersed, and regular business at the hotel's front desk resumed.

"Ah, yes, Mr. Hollister," said Hingham, "we've been expecting you. Are you alone?"

"My wife will be arriving later in the weekend. That is, if she doesn't stay at another hotel closer to the ritzy shops."

Hingham chuckled. "Very well, if you'll just sign here. I do apologize for the disturbance. This simply does not happen at the Palace. In fact, I can say without the slightest fear of contradiction that the Palace Hotel is considered by *tout le monde* to be the *ne plus ultra* of hotels. We owe you and Dr. Verne here an apology."

Mr. Hingham liked to show off his French. It made him feel sophisticated and cosmopolitan, and to do so in front of a famous Frenchman made him feel especially clever.

Hollister was not impressed. "Don't worry about us," he snapped. "That young man there lost his life. Finding his killer is more important than discommoding a few guests. I hope your house dick is a good one."

"Uh, yes. Yes, you're quite right, Mr. Hollister. You have such a colorful way of speaking, sir, if I may say so. So . . . *recherché,* as it were. In fact, the French have an expression . . ."

"Tu pêtes plus haut de ton cul," Jake Hollister said.

Jules Verne broke into a loud, surprised guffaw.

Jaw dropping, Hingham was mystified to hear French coming out of a Texan. "W-what did you say?"

"Just a phrase I picked up from a French girl I used to run around with."

Verne laughed all the louder.

Hingham knew when he was being twitted. He slapped the key on the desk and said primly, "I will have both you gentlemen's bags sent up to your rooms as soon as we get the situation straightened out in the lobby."

Hingham, whose French had come out of school-books and novels, could hardly have been expected to understand that Jake Hollister had alleged, in earthy Parisian slang, that Hingham (literally translated) farted higher than his anus, by which he meant to convey that Hingham was a pompous fool.

"Your key, Dr. Verne. Here is yours, Mr. Hollister. The manager picked it out especially for you. One of our better rooms."

"Thank you."

Hollister walked with Jules Verne into the pride of the Palace's lobby: one of its latest-model, steam-operated Otis elevators. The operator had stepped outside to talk to the dispatcher.

"Where on earth did you learn *patois*?" Verne asked, still grinning. Then the grin faded, and his brow furrowed. "Pardon, but you look familiar."

The other man checked to see if anyone was looking, then lifted the edge of what was apparently a brunet wig, showing blond hair. "I'm not Hollister. Tom Olam, of the Bavarian Secret Service. We've met before, Dr. Verne."

Tom and Verne had met at the signing of the Second Compact, the grand European alliance against Bismarck's Prussia.

"Olam! But why this ruse?"

"Undercover. Our organization has an interest in this convention of the so-called 'World Science League.' For one thing, we've never heard of it before."

"Neither had I until I received an invitation," Verne said. "But it seemed quite the legitimate affair. I was looking forward to meeting some of my colleagues from around the world. Why is your organization suspicious?"

"Well, the list of invitees is a roster of some of the world's best and most eccentric scientific minds. Masterminds. Some are quite legitimate and are on the side of law and order, like yourself. Others are a bit ambivalent, and still others are beyond the pale. But there's more to it. We have reason to believe that the convention is a front for a mass meeting of the World Crime League. Some of the globe's most notorious criminal masterminds have checked into this hotel over the past two days."

"You have seen them?"

"Other operatives have. They've observed not the masterminds themselves, but their henchmen, many of whom we have dossiers on."

"I see. Whom do you—"

Verne was interrupted by the elevator operator, a thin young man walking back into the car. The men suspended conversation until the operator let them off on Verne's floor. Tom led the way out and down the hall as Verne spoke in a hushed tone.

"Whom do you suspect is attending this affair?"

"We know Moriarty is here. Haven't seen him, but I have a suspicion that the man who died had a run-in with one of his goons. He was an operative, too. Jarvis Gresham, of the American Secret Service."

"Why did they kill him?"

Tom shrugged. "His cover may have been blown. We might never find out."

"Who else is here, may I ask?"

"Operatives, or criminals?"

"Both."

"Well, just about every intelligence outfit in the world has a representative here. As for notorious masterminds, there's Dr. Kondor, Count Cagliostro, and Lord Yosho Tomino, all the way from Japan. Robur is rumored to make an appearance."

"Robur! *Mon Dieu!*"

"And there are others, many others. It's a real meeting of masterminds. Nemo is here."

"Ah, Nemo, my favorite genius. I do hope he has not reverted to his anarchist ways."

"No, we think he's OK."

"And what—oh, here's my room. Why don't you come in, Mr. Olam."

"'Hollister,' please."

"Sorry. Do come in."

Verne opened the door and let 'Hollister' pass through.

"Tell me, how did you come to undertake this impersonation? I must tell you I was looking forward to meeting the real Jake Hollister."

"It's a long story. Hollister got an invitation but smelled something fishy. He alerted his government, which was negotiating with us for certain technological data; to make a long story short, they offered his undercover 'part' to me, since I'm also American."

Verne was looking out the window at the hilly skyline of San Francisco. "Magnificent. The city has grown up overnight, they tell me. Remarkable! But this region is known for violent earthquakes. Sad to think that one day San Francisco might be doomed to destruction." Verne turned from the window. "Tell me, Mr. Olam, you must have some idea what it's all about, this so-called convention."

Walking to the windows, Tom Olam shrugged. "All we know is that something big is up. We have a vague suspicion—just a suspicion—of who's behind it all. Room's a little stuffy, don't you think? No use waiting till the bellboy gets here."

Tom drew back the curtains and threw open all the windows to let in the city air. By the modern standards that Tom was used to, it was as pure as a breeze through a forest glade, the only thing tainting it the faint smell of horse manure.

"Professor Moriarty?"

"Perhaps. But it could be the reputed mastermind of all masterminds, the criminal's criminal. A shadowy figure. We don't even have a name for him."

"Ah, 'The Master.' I thought he was the stuff of legend only."

"We could be wrong. Perhaps it is Moriarty. Or even Robur. Maybe either or both want to enlist allies to rule the world."

"I appreciate your telling me this," Verne said. "And I hope you will keep me abreast of developments."

"Be happy to, though I suspect I'll be quite busy this weekend."

"No doubt."

"Nevertheless, we'll keep in touch," Tom said. "Please be very careful, Dr. Verne. This hotel could be a dangerous place over the next few days. If you wish to contact me, send a message to Room 212."

"I will be careful. Good-bye, Mr. Olam."

Tom closed the door quietly and looked up and down the hall. The coast was clear.

He looked at his key. It was marked 613. Better check it out before going down to 212, where the Countess Marianne, who'd checked in a week ago under the name of Lady Ada Lovelace, was waiting for him.

He walked briskly to the end of the hall, went through a door, mounted a service stairway, and went up two flights, remembering the floor plan from his briefing sessions. He exited the stairwell and moved left toward a door just down from what looked like a service elevator.

"'One of our better rooms,'" Tom grumbled.

A man approached, and he was instantly recognizable: a shock of hair, bushy mustache, string tie, white suit. The only thing that threw Tom momentarily was that he was so young. Here was a much younger Samuel Clemens than is usually pictured. A veteran newspaperman, he was a noted figure in this alternate California; in fact, he was the official of the "Emperor" of the state.

"Good day to you, sir," Clemens said in passing.

"Good afternoon," Tom said, and watched him amble down the hall. Mark Twain had to exist in every universe where there were great rivers.

Tom opened the door and went in. The curtains were drawn, but enough light leaked through to illumine a resplendent room, walls of damask, rugs of Persia, furniture by Chippendale, Hepplewhite, Sheraton, and Phyfe. Worth millions in the era Tom came from. On this date in the history of this alternate universe known as Castle Falkenstein, this steampunk-ersatz nineteenth century, it was still worth a neat nickel, even though they were a hundred years less antiqued.

"This will do," Tom said. He took off his suit coat and threw it on the canopied bed.

Come to think of it, though, the place was a little small to be appointed this lavishly. Well, they'd said there'd been a change of management. Maybe an economy move?

Every time Tom checked into a hotel room in this era—which corresponded to the year 1875 in his home universe (the universe of World War One, Two, and Almost-Three, of rock and roll and pizza and rap music and Rollerblades, and in which Castle Falkenstein had never been built)—he had to remind himself that there were indeed bathrooms in the best hotel rooms. They did not have flush toilets. They had commodes, the kind that must be emptied by the chamber maids. But it amounted more or less to the same convenience.

Yeesh, it was dark in here. But a certain urgency impelled him to a polished door in the right wall. He opened it and rushed on through.

"Yahhhhhhh!"

His yell echoed in an immense darkness, and he found himself hanging onto the doorknob, dangling from a vertiginous height in an elevator shaft that looked bottomless. Eight stories, only eight, Tom told himself as he tried to reach for the door frame . He caught his left hand on a metal ridge, but it slipped off and he nearly lost his precarious grip on the knob. He tried again. The door's hinges, never designed to withstand 170 pounds of hanging, desperate secret agent, creaked worrisomely.

Using his right foot, Tom pushed off against the wall of the concrete shaft and managed to swing the door and himself back far enough so that he could get an arm up over the sill. Risking a fall, but confident of his upper-body strength, he let go of the doorknob and hauled himself up to safety.

He stretched out on the thick carpeting for a moment to get his breath. Then he got to his feet and closed the polished door.

"Sure is nice furniture," he said, leaving the room.

Two

A BEAUTIFUL YOUNG woman opened the door to Room 212.

"Good evening, Lady Lovelace," Tom greeted her.

"Come in, Mr. Hollister," the woman said. "You are a married man, but I've always wanted to make love to you. Kiss me. Then you can do anything you want with me."

"OK."

A little later, they were lounging on the settee in the plush suite's sitting room, having tea.

"You play an English lady well," Tom said. "But I guess as a real countess, it isn't so hard."

The Countess Marianne Theresa Desiree shrugged. "It's a good thing my English is British and not American."

"Your English is fine when you want it to be. I wish we'd been able to contact Lady Lovelace to make sure she wasn't coming to this thing."

Marianne shrugged. "She's been known to disappear for long periods."

"I hope she's still not mixed up with the Temple of Ra. She's one mysterious lady. Anyway, if she does show up, you have your backup cover as Jake Hollister's wife."

"I don't like playing wives. How did things go with checking in?"

"I almost didn't make it back from my room," Tom said.

"Trouble?"

"Not a lot, but it was touch and go there for a minute." Tom told her about the bathroom with the surprise.

"Nasty trick. But how was it done?"

"The hotel was recently bought from the original owners, who built it. Whoever the new owners are, they cut a door into that wall. As to why they gave me that room, I may have been recognized. Unless someone is trying to kill Jacob Hollister." Tom took a sip of tea and bit into a social tea biscuit. "Boy, was I suckered. I should have known there couldn't be anything on the other side of that wall but the shaft. But I didn't get the joke until it was almost too late."

"Some joke. Who do you think killed the American Secret Service man, the same people who cut the false door?"

"I doubt it. You saw two of Moriarty's goons check in. Did you see Jarvis take their bags?"

"No, some traveling salesman started talking to me. Before I shooed him away, they had gone up. Then you arrived, and I left the lobby. I missed the whole thing."

"Well, Jarvis was undercover as a bellhop, and Jarvis came back shot. In any event, Moriarty's goons being here means Moriarty is somewhere about. It was a mistake to do it, though, killing him. It's not Moriarty's style. But the house detective is a stooge, and the shooting will probably go unreported. I'm pretty sure if we inquired at the desk, they'd say, 'What shooting?' Meanwhile, this entire hotel may be booby-trapped."

"Was Verne the last of the convention attendees?" the countess asked.

"The last of the good guys. I think there're more baddies to arrive yet. Funny thing is, I checked with the Americans and they've not spotted one underworld figure yet. Henchmen, yes, but no actual masterminds."

Marianne took a paper from a nearby trivet table. "Let's see who we have confirmed, on the basis of known henchmen. Cagliostro, Kondor, Baron von Brass, Dr. Manchu, Moriarty, Lord Tomino, Dr. Lovelorn. . . . Am I missing anyone?"

"Nemo."

"You're counting him among the bad ones?"

"No . . . but to tell the truth I've never trusted him. Is this the program schedule for the convention?"

"Yes."

"Quite a full slate here," Tom commented, unfolding the sheets. He read:

WELCOME TO THE FIRST ANNUAL CONVENTION OF THE WORLD SCIENCE LEAGUE. WE DO HOPE YOU FIND AT LEAST SOME OF OUR FUNCTIONS OF INTEREST AND USE TO YOU THIS WEEKEND. ENJOY YOUR STAY IN SAN FRANCISCO.

Friday Evening
  5:30 PM, Opening Ceremonies. Keynote Speech by Professor Julian Morris of Stanford University. "Toward a World Ruled by Science and Sanity."

  6 PM, Grand Ballroom. Meet Your Colleagues Party. (Use the ticket issued with your convention packet to get a complimentary cocktail!)

  7 PM, Dinner Hour. The Palace's Presidio Dining Room features fine cuisine in the tradition of Old California. Try the Salada Española!

8 PM, Embarcadero Room. Panel Discussion, "Mad Science: Threat or Opportunity?" Dr. Jules Verne, Dr. Jeckyll, Dr. Victor Frankenstein, Captain Nemo.

9 PM, Gold Rush Room. Panel Discussion, "Rule by Scientist: Plato's Republic or Technocratic Tyranny?" Dr. Jules Verne, Charles Babbage, Richard von Ruppelt.

"Totally bogus," Tom said. "This isn't the real program. The real one's going to be conducted in secret meetings all over the hotel, in private rooms."

"What is on the real program?" Marianne asked.

"I dunno. World domination workshops. Panel discussions on developing an evil plot that really works."

"*Vraiment?*"

"Doubt it'll be that formal. I do know this place will be seething with clandestine get-togethers. Master criminals from all over the world will be forging alliances, cutting deals, carving up territories. But I'm not sure even all that's the real purpose of this shindig."

"*Qu'est-ce que c'est, le* 'shindig'?"

"*Fête.* We're not onto the real purpose yet. We have to penetrate the inner circle, somehow. If only electronics existed. We could bug a few rooms."

"Bug? We put insects in the rooms?"

"No, eavesdrop."

"But we can do that without the insects."

Tom shook his head skeptically. "I don't know if ordinary surveillance techniques are going to work in this den of geniuses. We could rent rooms next to people, put our earphones up against the walls, and listen to an entire prerecorded conversation filled with nothing but trivia."

"Prerecorded? They can do that?"

"Tricks, clever tricks. All these mad scientist types are enormously resourceful and deviously clever. And the criminals are master criminals. They didn't become so by getting caught easily."

Marianne shrugged. "So, we have to be smarter."

Tom sighed. "I should go down to the desk and demand a new room."

"Will you change character?"

Tom shook his head. "I'm going to continue the Hollister role for a while. They may know I'm not Hollister, but it might do well to simply play along, pretend that nothing's happened. I won't even mention the trick bathroom at the desk. Wouldn't do me any good if I did. Keeping mum about it might confuse the hell out of them. Are you ready to attend that cocktail party as Lady Ada Lovelace, math and computer whiz?"

"I'm rather looking forward to it, darling," Marianne said in her best British upper-class accent.

Tom grinned. "Hey, that's pretty good. If you work on your American accent, you could play my wife. On the other hand, you don't strike me as the Western corn-fed beauty type. Features are too delicate."

"You don't strike me as the cattle baron/inventor type."

"What type do I strike you as?"

"The handsome soldier type." She kissed him.

"Thanks. I kind of like you, too."

"Tout a l'heure, mon cher. Give me some time for my *toilette.* I want flirt with as many men as I can at the party."

"Now, see, this is the part of secret agent work that makes me a little uncomfortable. I don't like the thought of you cozying up to these megalomaniac types."

Marianne gave him a haughty stare. "You don't think I can take care of myself?"

"I know you can take care of yourself. I was just feeling sorry for the megalomaniacs."

She threw a social tea biscuit at him as he dashed to the bedroom door.

TOM CHECKED HIS adopted personality in the mirror, making sure his own long blond hair was up and out of sight under the wig. He ascertained that his spirit-gum mustache, which added a dashing accent, was on straight. He had changed suits, and this one had an even flashier cowboy cut. The string tie with the diamonds-in-silver buckle lent an unmistakable Texas flair.

His next task was to make contact with the American undercover agents. He intended to do that at the cocktail party.

Just about every intelligence organization in the world had operatives at this convention. The Prussians were here, too, Tom was fairly sure. Even they had a stake in a plot to widen the tentacled reach of the World Crime League throughout the globe.

Tom had a hunch that, for once, the Prussians weren't behind it all. Bismarck, their "Iron Chancellor," was a nasty, hard-nosed SOB with designs of his own, but even he would balk at outright criminality. Well, in principle. Maybe.

No, in all this—the convention and its bubble and boil of plot and intrigue—Tom got a distinct whiff of something very, very strange. But he had no idea what it was.

He checked himself over once again. He looked OK.

He walked into the next room, where Marianne was still busy at her *toilette*, sitting at the makeup table.

"Just another minute, dear," she said.

It took her fifteen. Tom killed the time reading a complimentary copy of The Atlantic Monthly. It ran a long piece by Herman Melville. The article was one Tom, a Melville enthusiast, was not familiar with.

Presently, Marianne announced, "Ready!"

"I was just thinking of starting on a serial."

A knock on the door interrupted Marianne's sarcastic reply. Tom answered the door. A bellhop.

"Message, sir."

Tom took the note and handed the boy a shiny nickel.

"Thanks, sir."

Dear Fellow Seeker of Truth,

You are invited to a private gathering of Men of Science tonight at 10 PM, Penthouse. Issues of Great Moment and Significance will be discussed. Refreshments will be served. No RSVP necessary.

Your Host

"Well, they sent it to this room, which means I'm being watched. Which means they probably know who we are."

"Then why did they leave me alone?" Marianne wondered.

"Don't know. But as far as the convention goes,

here's the real program," Tom said, handing the note to Marianne.

Marianne read it. "Are there no women of science?"

"You know, Marianne, you're the only woman in this world I can think of who'd make a comment like that. Are you sure you weren't born in my world?"

"Oh, yes, in the English 'men' includes women, but I still think it's not right. I get—the way you say it— 'pissed off' when they use it. I could kill them."

"I know. I'll speak to them about it. I don't want you killing anyone we don't need to kill. Wouldn't do, leaving all those bodies around. Messy. Are you ready now, or can I start on this sea adventure novel?"

"Watch no one finds your messy body," Marianne said darkly, pushing Tom out the door.

Three

HE "MEET YOUR Colleagues" party was
lightly attended. To Tom, the room was full
of strangers. He could not guess who they
were or what they were doing at the party. Most of
the males in the crowd had an academic look: spec-
tacles, beards, tweed suits, sweater vests. Slightly
scruffy, most of them, the clothes a bit threadbare
and seedy. The women were a bit too well-dressed,
though, and Tom thought he detected an air of the
demimondaine about them.

Tom guessed that many of these "scientists" had
been pulled in off the street.

Tom spied Verne in a corner. He was seated in a
hard-back chair, a cocktail glass in his hand, looking forlorn. Tom walked over and spoke briefly with

him, then beckoned for Marianne to join them. Having just prepared Verne for the ruse, Tom introduced her as Lady Ada Lovelace, the brilliant mathematician and colleague of Charles Babbage. Verne rose, bowed, and kissed Marianne's hand. He knew Marianne, but played along nicely. When dealing with the Bavarian Secret Service, Verne knew to expect the unexpected, and Tom had counted on that.

"So nice to see you again," Verne said.

"You look so sad and lonely," Marianne said, in character.

"Where is everybody?" Verne asked. "I see no one here I know, or would want to know."

She said, "Didn't you get an invitation to a private party?"

"Yes. Is that where everyone will be? Who are these people, anyway? Do you know any of them?"

Tom casually scanned the room. "No. They're window-dressing, probably. Remember, this weekend's not what it's cracked up to be."

"I think I understand that expression. Yes, it is obviously a sham." Verne rose. "Well, what shall we do?"

"Kill time until the meeting. What do you say the three of us have dinner?"

"I would be delighted," Verne said.

That evening, the Presidio Room's seafood special was red snapper in a spicy wine sauce.

"This was wonderful," Marianne said. "For American food."

"Definitely," Tom said, finishing the last of it. Nobody had gotten around to commenting on the food until Marianne's comment. Dinner conversation, mostly between Tom and Verne, had ranged from Verne's fiction to the latest developments in ironclad dreadnoughts to Verne's duties as France's science minister, in which office he was a key figure in the Second Compact, the alliance forged between certain European powers and the faerie Seelie against the designs of Bismarck and the Unseelie.

The break in the conversation caused Tom to reflect on how different this universe was from the one he came from. Here, Germany was not united and, if King Ludwig of Bavaria had anything to say about it, never would be. Thus, in the next century, there would be no First World War, and no Second World War either—and all that that entailed. No mass destruction, no slaughter of millions, and—afterward—no Cold War or danger of a nuclear war.

"Excellent," Verne said. "I did not expect to find such cuisine so far from civilization."

"San Francisco is a little isolated," Tom said, "come to think of it. But not much. Even though Texas and California are republics, the English-speaking culture on the continent still stretches from sea to shining sea, linked up by railroads and telegraph lines."

"I understand that the United States is negotiating with the Indians to allow telegraph cables and railroads to pass through the Indian nation. Do you think the Indians will permit it?"

"Maybe," Tom said, "but the Iron Horse is still a big bugbear to the Indians."

"Symbolic, no doubt. Ah, but they must realize, sooner or later, that science and technology are universal. They are not the exclusive province of any one group of people."

"I think they realize that. But their attitude toward such things is quite different from ours."

"No doubt."

"Excuse me, Dr. Verne?"

"Eh?"

It was a busboy, a young man with a sallow complexion. "A note just came to the desk for you. They said it was urgent."

"A note, for me? Do you have it?"

"No, sir. The sender said it was very confidential, and the manager has to give it to you personally."

"But I am having dinner," Verne protested.

"Sorry, sir, I was asked to apologize. The message is urgent."

"Urgent? What could be urgent here? Very well, I will come."

"Thank you, sir." The young man walked away. Tom noticed that his gait was a little strange. Something awkward about it. Gimp leg, no doubt.

"I do hope it's not bad news from home," Verne said. "I wonder if a mail ship came in."

"He said a note, I believe," Tom said, "not a letter."

"I'll be back directly," Verne said. He left the dining room.

"I don't like this," Tom said. "But it would look funny if I accompanied Verne. You want dessert?"

"I can do without it. But he just went out to the lobby, didn't he?"

"Tom craned his neck, trying to get a view beyond the pillars just outside the door. "I can't see the desk. It'll be all right, I guess. Pretty sure. Let's have some dessert."

Ten minutes later, when Verne had not yet returned, Tom was not so sure. They left their apple strudels half eaten and rushed out into the lobby. Verne was nowhere in sight. The man at the desk, whey-faced and gaunt, yet another hotel employee with anemia or a vitamin deficiency or whatever the problem was around here, knew nothing about a message for a Dr. Verne.

"Are you absolutely sure?" Tom insisted. "The busboy said the manager wanted to hand-deliver the note."

"I'm sorry, Mr. Sextus isn't in at the moment."

"Who?"

"Mr. Sextus is the manager, sir. Would you like to leave a message for him?"

"We're looking for Dr. Verne. He's missing."

"Uh . . . how long has he been missing, sir? Have you checked his room?"

Tom smiled. "Hey, never thought of that. Sorry to be a pest."

"Is there anything else I can do, sir?"

"Yes. Please take a message for Dr. Verne. Tell him to get in touch with me as soon as possible. Please."

"Certainly, sir."

As they were waiting for the elevator, Tom shook his head.

"Sextus. What the hell kind of name is that, especially when the house dick is named Quintus? Something's screwy in this place."

"What do you think it is?"

"Wish I knew. Here's the elevator."

They went up, exited the elevator, and walked to Room 308.

"Knocking might attract attention. If he's in there, we owe him an apology, but let's just go in."

Tom flipped over his left lapel and fished a skeleton key from a tiny pocket in the back of it. Wriggling this tool in the keyhole, he made short work of unlocking the door. He re-hid the key and slowly pushed the door open.

They walked into the plush sitting room, a match for Marianne's. Also a twin was the connecting door to the bedroom. This door opened, and out walked a tall, muscular man.

"Hello, there," he said.

Another man, shorter and stockier, followed him through the door. Marianne recognized both at once from the lobby. Tom knew their faces from police photos. Both were goons on Moriarty's payroll.

"How did you two get in here?" Tom demanded.

"We might ask the same of you."

"I still want to know."

"We have a key."

"That's a lie," Tom said. "What's going on? Talk. What are your names?"

"I'm Slocum. Jim Slocum. Pleased to meetcha."

"You ask too many questions," the other one said.

"I have another question for you," Marianne said. "What have you done with Dr. Verne?"

Slocum laughed. "Hear that, Jean-Claude? She has questions, too. That's pretty funny."

"Yeah, that's funny," Jean-Claude said flatly.

"We were sent up here by Dr. Verne," Slocum said.

"Impossible," Marianne said.

"To do what?" Tom asked pointedly.

"To fetch some papers of his."

"What papers?" Tom asked.

Slocum's gaze took in the sitting room in one big sweep, then alighted on something. He grinned. "There they are."

Tom turned to see a leather portfolio on the end table next to the settee.

Slocum crossed the room and picked it up. "Yeah. These papers. Didn't see them before."

"Where you going?" Jean-Claude asked, stiff-arming Tom as he tried to step into the bedroom.

"I'm going to see who's in that bedroom. Any objections?"

"Yeah, I object."

"Want that arm broken?"

"Hey, don't mess around with Jean-Claude," Slocum warned. "He has a nasty temper."

"So do I," Tom said, grabbing Jean-Claude's hand and twisting it in a painfully wrong direction.

Jean-Claude yelped and jumped back, nursing his wrist.

"You know, Hollister, for a guy what breaks and enters into hotel rooms, you're pretty damn pushy."

"That's Mr. Hollister to you, gorilla-face."

"Oh, excuse me. Mr. Hollister. You know, you don't strike me as a Texan. You ain't got enough cow shit on your boots."

Slocum reached out and grabbed Marianne by the hair and yanked her toward him; at the same time his hand reached into his coat and drew out a knife from behind his back. The blade went to Marianne's throat.

"Get out or I ventilate her windpipe."

But it was Slocum who lost his wind as Marianne's elbow made a depression in his diaphragm. Slocum's face registered a mixture of pain and surprise. He was even more surprised to find himself flying through the air and crashing into a glass-front highboy. The glass shattered, the highboy went low, and so did Slocum.

But he recovered quickly, picked himself out of the wreckage, and grinned.

"Hey, that was some move, lady," he said almost admiringly.

Then he charged.

A donnybrook ensued. Objects flew, furniture disintegrated. Tom and Jean-Claude tussled while Marianne threw Slocum around the room, when she wasn't kicking him in the head, midsection, and posterior. He tried for the fallen knife several times, and once got several fingers broken.

Jean-Claude liked to kick-box, and Tom indulged him. Jean-Claude was rather adept at the whirling kick. Tom admired his form, but he also liked the way Jean-Claude went tumbling on his backside when Tom came up under the kick with a shove to the back of the thigh.

"Your legs're too short for that savate stuff," Tom told him.

Jean-Claude picked up a hard-back chair and charged. Tom hooked a trivet table with a foot, shoved it into his path, and stepped aside to watch Jean-Claude injure himself grievously as he went sprawling. The stocky Frenchman yowled, writhing on the floor, holding his right shin. Tom turned to help Marianne, but she was doing such a fine job dislocating Slocum's left shoulder that he didn't want to interrupt her.

However, the door opened, and Quintus rushed in.

"What's going on here?" he demanded.

The fight stopped. Marianne let go of Slocum's arm and stepped away.

Tom said, "We found these men in Dr. Verne's room."

"And just exactly what are you doing in Dr. Verne's room?" The curious thing about Quintus's voice was that it carried unmistakable overtones of menace while remaining totally flat.

"Looking for him. He's missing."

"I just saw him downstairs," Quintus said. "I ought to arrest you for breaking and entering."

"What about these two?"

"Dr. Verne sent us up," Slocum said. "We have a key." He reached into a pocket gingerly and, wincing, brought out a hotel key. "Ouch. She broke my damn finger. I want to file charges against this woman."

"They're lying," Tom said. "They probably abducted Verne. He's probably in the bedroom right there. Why don't you take a look, Quintus?"

"I don't have to take a look," Quintus said. "I told you I just saw Dr. Verne downstairs. He's about to take part in a panel discussion in the Embarcadero Room, off the lobby. You can go down and see him yourself. I suggest you do that. If not. . . ."

Quintus eased open the front of his jacket to reveal the butt of a pistol sticking out of a shoulder holster.

"If not, I am prepared to deal with you very severely."

"OK, we'll leave," Tom said. "Just dropped in to say hello. See you guys later. Thanks for showing us those judo moves."

"Yeah," Slocum said, massaging his shoulder. "Any time."

"You'll be billed for the damages," Quintus added as Tom and Marianne passed him on their way out.

"Do you take American Express?"

Four

VERNE WAS NOT present in the Embarcadero Room. An empty place at the panel table was marked with a paper sign bearing his name. Looking over the other panelists, Tom saw two unfamiliar faces behind familiar name signs. Tom had never had occasion to meet Dr. Henry Jekyll (or Mr. Hyde, for that matter, for in this universe Dr. Jekyll had managed to suppress his dark alter ego). Victor Frankenstein was also a stranger. But the bloke in the uniform looked like the Captain Nemo Tom knew, and on whose undersea vessel Tom had spent a harrowing two weeks, some time ago. However, something about the way Nemo looked was strange, but Tom couldn't put a finger on it.

Tom scanned the audience. There was not a face he recognized.

Then he leaned toward Marianne and whispered, "I'm beginning to suspect that this thing is even more of a bamboozle that we first thought."

Marianne arched her eyebrows. "Bamboozle?"

"Sham. Show. A fake."

"Why did they do it?"

"I dunno, but they have Verne. That may have been the idea all along, but I can't figure out why they made this elaborate production out of it."

"They lure him to San Francisco because it is out of the way?"

"Could be. But maybe this is a real meeting of criminal minds, as well. A forging of an alliance between the straight-out thugs and the mad scientists. Presided over by the Moriarty types, who are both."

"That makes sense."

"Maybe they wanted to lure as many scientists of whatever allegiance, to recruit them. But not many bothered to come. The ones we see here are probably ringers."

"Ringers?"

"Impostors. I have my doubts about Nemo."

"He looks like Nemo."

"But he has the same strange look that everyone has around here. Weird. Can't put my finger on it, though. Too bad we couldn't get hold of Nemo to ask him if he was coming to this thing."

"People on undersea boats are hard to get hold of."

"This is true. Oops, here comes someone we're sure of. Von Ruppelt."

Richard von Ruppelt, inventor of the extraordinary weapon known as the magnetic ray projector, slunk into the room. He was wont to slink, von Ruppelt was. A reticent sort for all his mastery of the more arcane forces of nature, he preferred to keep a low public profile. Although a member in good standing of the Bavarian court, he was an American citizen, having been born in New York City of an American mother by a German father.

"Talk of strange-looking people," Marianne whispered.

"Shush, he's a friend."

Tom had to agree that von Ruppelt looked the part of the mad scientist. Totally bald, hatchet-faced, and horse-toothed, beady eyes made even smaller behind thick spectacle lenses, Ruppelt was, to say the least, an unprepossessing figure. In fact, Tom had to admit, he was downright creepy.

But a real nice guy.

Now, if somebody said that aloud, Tom thought, *I'd burst out laughing.*

Actually it was true. Ruppelt, as charming a man as you would ever want to meet, sidled over to where Tom and Marianne were sitting and took a seat a discreet distance away, but he acknowledged them with a sidelong glance and a half-grin. Tom wished he hadn't. He wasn't supposed to know Hollister.

But then again, Tom thought further, they could have met at the mixer. OK, fine.

Keep on your toes, Tom told himself. These webs of deception do get tangled.

"Where's Verne?" Ruppelt asked out of the side of his mouth.

"Don't know. Kidnapped, maybe."

Ruppelt did a double take. "What?"

Came a voice from the back of the room, "Ah, there you are, Dr. Verne!"

Everyone turned. Someone Tom didn't know was shaking hands with Verne, who had just come through the double doors. Smiling and looking hale and healthy, Verne walked to the dais, shook hands with the other panelists, and took a seat at the table.

"OK, I confess," Tom murmured to Marianne. "I don't know what the hell is going on."

"Neither do I."

Ruppelt was giving Tom an odd look. With a sheepish grin, Tom shrugged apologetically.

The panel discussion, moderated by Verne, began. After introducing himself, Verne launched into a short introductory talk on the nature of scientific progress in history. It was short and to the point, but not in any sense comprehensive or conclusive, leaving open wide areas for further discussion. To Tom, Verne seemed as eloquent as ever, and as voluble, self-assured, and optimistic. The only thing that did not track was. . . .

Oh, no, Tom thought.

The weirdness. The whatever the hell it was. Verne had it, too.

This was getting annoying. Tom cudgeled his brain, trying desperately to put into words what it was about too many people he'd seen this weekend.

"Marianne."

"Hm?"

"Don't you notice something about Verne? Something different?"

Marianne took a few moments to look and analyze. At length, she said, "Yes."

"OK. What is it?"

She took an equal amount of time to think about it.

"I don't know," she finally said.

Tom sighed.

Dr. Henry Jekyll, a mild-mannered fellow with saintly eyes, introduced himself, made a few comments on Verne's speechlet, and passed the ball to Victor Frankenstein, who also looked the part of the mad scientist, though not in the comic-book way von Ruppelt did. Frankenstein had one of those faces that are a boon to the men who own them, perennially young and good-looking, the kind to which women are instantly attracted. But there was something positively psychotic gleaming in the depths of those steel-blue eyes.

Not the kind of guy you'd like to room with in college, Tom thought. He'd steal your women, and maybe your brain.

Next to talk was Nemo, who broached the subject of the scientist as hero. The voice was Nemo's, the style of speech was his, but the substance of what he said seemed to Tom predigested, perhaps taken whole out of a textbook. Then, having come to his point, Nemo simply stopped talking. An awkward silence fell.

Verne made an innocuous comment, and the panel discussion continued. It was not at all interesting. Verne seemed to have shot his bolt in the opening speech, for he did not have much that was provocative to say after that. Frankenstein took up the slack by rambling on and on without ever coming to a point. Jekyll did not say much at all.

Tom tried to draw a look from Verne, but failed. However, Verne did not seem to be avoiding Tom's and Marianne's gaze. Tom got the impression that Verne was simply oblivious to the people he'd walked out on.

"Think Verne might have had a stroke?" Tom said sotto voce.

Marianne shrugged. "Stroke? But he'd be sick."

"I was thinking of a . . . oh, never mind. Just grasping at straws. Something happened to him. He hasn't so much as noticed that we're here."

"Maybe we said something to offend him?"

"What, though? Can you think of anything?"

Marianne shook her head. "I can't understand it."

"I'd like to leave and come back when this is over, but I don't want to let Verne get out of sight."

"Want me to stay? What exactly do you want to do?"

"Take a pee."

"Oh. Urgent? OK, I'll stay."

"I hate to leave, but . . . well, you know."

"I know, I know," said Marianne. "I have to make the excuse soon, too."

"Well, we both shouldn't leave at once."

"Get going, be back quick."

"As quick as you can make it in 1875."

Tom got up and left the hall. Verne's eyes did not follow him out, Tom noticed, though Nemo's did. Strange thing.

Ever since he'd been spellnapped (the only word that applied) into this strangely altered nineteenth century, Tom Olam had been continually surprised by the early appearances of some technological devel-

opments. Elevators, for one. The first true public pas-
senger elevators, steam-powered, had come along in
the 1850s in this universe. He wasn't sure about back
home. The same applied to indoor plumbing.
Although it would be a while before flush toilets came
into wide use, there were many low-tech ways of
accomplishing the same task. The hotel, for instance,
had an absolutely palatial men's room of marble and
stone and terra-cotta, off the lobby, with ranks of commodes and urinals that used the same flow of water
to carry the raw discharge into a local sewerage system (which emptied raw smack into the bay, of
course, these being pre-environmentalist times).

No technological wonder. The ancient Romans
had better. But it would do in a pinch, Tom thought,
as he stepped briskly to the door with an engraved
marble lintel reading LAVATORY—GENTLEMEN.

A man in coveralls came out and held up a hand.

"Sorry, sir, cleaning."

"Oh, damn. Is there another one?"

"Only the Ladies'. Sorry."

"S'okay."

He'd have to run up to Marianne's room.

The elevator operator, yet another pallid-faced
youth, was waiting for him, perched on his tiny seat,
one hand on the control lever.

"Three, please."

"Yes, sir."

The doors closed. Then the elevator went down.

"Yo," Tom said. "Up, please."

"Sorry, sir. Have to go down first. Cable problems."

"Cable problems?"

"Yes, sir. Knots in the cable. Have to go down and unwind all the way before we go up."

"Uh-huh. Make it quick, OK, pal?"

"Yes, sir, right away, sir."

Knots in the cable? Tom scowled to himself. Sounds kind of scary. Never heard of such a thing.

Well, this was 1875.

The elevator dropped three levels and stopped. The kid opened the doors, revealing a basement that resembled, speaking of Rome, the ancient catacombs.

"Where the hell are we?" Tom demanded.

"Basement, sir. Be just a minute."

"Look, I'm in a hurry. Take me back to the lobby. I'll take the stairs."

"Be just a minute, sir."

The kid sat there, staring vacantly off into space, hand still on the control lever. Tom shuffled his feet and coughed, wishing for a cigar or something to light up. But he didn't smoke, never had.

"Just what are you waiting for?"

"For the engineer to tell me it's OK to go up."

"Well, where is he? I don't want to make trouble, kid, but I really have an urgent need. . . ."

"Here he comes."

Footsteps outside. A bald, portly man in filthy overalls appeared and crooked a finger at the operator.

"I need you."

The operator got up and left the car, following the bald man. Tom stepped out to watch them walk off into the gloom. They went through a door to the right. The door closed, and Tom was alone.

Silence fell.

Whistling in the dark, Tom paced a few steps. Then he decided to see where the door went. He walked to it, opened it, and despaired at the long empty corridor, dark at both extremities, that confronted him. He closed the door and walked back to the elevator.

Well, he'd never run an elevator in his life, but how difficult could it be? He'd never hijacked an elevator before, either, but he was not going to be shanghaied to the cellar.

The control lever was gone.

"Uh-huh," Tom said.

Right. Now he would look for stairs. To the left, through a concrete archway, down a long tunnel? No, nothing but more darkness. He needed a torch. After rummaging through piles of debris here and there he had a stick, its end wrapped with some rags. No accelerant, but it was better than nothing. A lucifer produced from an inside pocket lighted the thing, and the gloom receded. He continued down the tunnel.

Stairs? No, a doorway to an empty room. He walked on, holding his torch. Another doorway made a blacker, oblong shape against the blackness, but this proved to be the mouth of another tunnel. He decided to turn into it.

He was about ten paces down its length when he began to hear footsteps behind him, heavy, hard-soled footfalls that echoed as if great weight had been brought down to make them.

Heart pounding, Tom increased his pace. The footfalls matched him. He began running, but the torch's flame sputtered and threatened to go out, so he cupped it with one hand as he ran. Whatever was chasing him broke into a sprint, closing fast.

Tom saw an intersecting tunnel cut through ahead and ducked down the left shaft, plunging into darkness. The torch picked that moment to go out, and Tom was running blind.

Yet he was not completely in the dark. Something gleamed ahead.

Stairs, light leaking through. He put on extra speed, but even as he leaped up the rickety stairs four steps at a time, the thing (it did not sound human) behind him always seemed only one flight behind him.

He ran up two flights, then a third, not daring to look behind. He could hear the thing panting and slavering. He kept clumping upward, wondering if he'd passed the lobby floor, but he kept shouting in his mind that stairs had to go somewhere, stairwells had to let out at some point. There was light up there, he could see it. This couldn't go on forever; but the chase seemed never-ending, and the beast behind him did not slacken its pace, had no thought of giving up its relentless pursuit. It wanted Tom, and it would get him.

The thing howled, and the sound of it froze Tom's heart.

A landing. Tom leaped the last five steps in one bound.

No door. A short corridor, a blank wall at its end. No door, no way out. The light came from a single, guttering candle in a sconce at the head of the stairs.

Tom reached into his coat and brought out a double-barreled derringer pistol. A popgun to shoot a monster. He reached his left hand inside his left boot and withdrew a knife. Retreating down the short cul-de-sac, he knelt and took up a firing position against the wall, keeping the knife in his left hand.

He took aim at a space just above the top of the last step, and waited. The footsteps had slowed; the thing's panting and burbling had subsided to a sound that was not unlike a soft chuckling. In fact, it sounded human. The footsteps clumped upward, slowly, more slowly. Whoever it was wore heavy, clumsy shoes.

And that is exactly what Tom saw stomping up the stairs, appearing at the top and coming to rest:

two heavy, brown leather work shoes, scuffed and begrimed.

Empty shoes.

Damn it, Tom thought, the hellish thing's invisible! Tom could see nothing in the flickering gloom.

There came a chortling that now sounded completely human, and a bit impish and derisive at that. Someone was having a jolly good joke. The candle guttered and nearly went out. Tom heard some general movement and unspecified noise.

He fired once, aiming for a spot above the shoes where a body would be. If there was a body.

Then he heard mocking laughter.

"Who are you?" Tom yelled.

"Who am I?" a man's voice answered. It was a well-bred voice, cultured and smooth. "I should think it obvious, my dear sir. Do I sound like a man?"

"Yes," Tom said.

"Can you see me?"

"No."

"Then, it quite follows that I am an invisible man."

"I see," Tom said. "Are you *the* Invisible Man?"

"The one and only."

"So pleased to meet you, Mr. Griffin," Tom said. "I've heard much about you."

"I'm flattered."

"What I heard was not flattering. Mind my asking a question?"

"Not at all."

"Why are you chasing me?"

"Chasing you? My dear sir, I merely wanted to speak to you."

"You could have done that easily. You chased me into this trap."

"Well, others were supposed to do that. Thugs, Moriarty's thugs, to be specific. I was half intending to warn you off, to get back into the elevator, and stay there. But you went running off at the first sound of my footsteps."

"Why didn't you say something? Or were you trying to frighten me to death?"

Griffin giggled. "I am sorry. I don't know what comes over me. I do love to give people a fright. It's one of the chief entertainments afforded by invisibility. I realize it's perverse, but I can't resist sometimes. Especially when I find a poor, timid soul walking the streets at night, alone. You've no idea how unnerving it is to hear footfalls following, and then turn around and see absolutely nothing. I can reduce even the most fearless night traveler to a gibbering hysteric within three blocks. It's ripping good fun."

"I'll wager. Who's in charge of this charade, by the way? Moriarty?"

"I don't know yet. It's all very mysterious."

"Whose side are you on?"

"Haven't quite decided," Griffin said. "I'll let you know. For the time being, however, and until I choose otherwise, I mean you no harm. Well, not much, anyway."

"How long have you been here in the hotel, Griffin? Who have you seen? Are you behind all this yourself?"

No answer.

"Griffin?"

Tom rose and walked to the top of the stairs. The boots still lay on the upper step. Tom passed a hand over them. Griffin was not in them. He must have stepped out before Tom had fired. Otherwise there would be a dead invisible man somewhere hereabouts.

Perhaps Tom had hit him? No, Griffin had doubtless seen the gun and jumped out of the work boots immediately.

Tom pocketed the gun and put the knife back into its boot sheath. No way to go but down. He started down the stairs, reached the first landing, and descended the next flight.

Suddenly, inexplicably, as if in some vicious carny fun house, the steps retracted into the floor, and the stairwell became a steep ramp, down which Tom slid on the seat of his pants all the way to the landing, which in turn tilted to become a ramp leading into a long, twisting chute, which Tom tumbled and slid down, slamming into the sides as it angled and turned. Finally, the turns stopped, and he scooted down one long, final incline and shot into free space. He fell.

"Damn!"

And fell, and fell.

Finally, he hit a soft and yielding mass and became deeply buried in a heap of something dry and soft and scratchy.

Straw. Smelly straw, reeking of horses. Coughing and choking, Tom thrashed upward, broke through the top of the heap, rolled away from the depression he'd made, and sat in the dark spitting dirty straw and picking it out of his eyes and hair.

Someone grabbed him from behind, and he felt cold steel against his Adam's apple.

"Don't move or I'll slit your throat," came a gruff voice into his ear.

Five

MARIANNE WAS BESIDE herself with indecision. She could not decide whether to go looking for Tom or to continue to wait for an opportunity to talk with Verne. The panel discussion still had fifteen minutes to run, and Tom had been gone almost a half hour. That was one long sojourn to the *pissoir,* Marianne thought.

And she had to go herself.

"Oh, bother," she grumbled, and got up and left the room. To hell with Verne. He would have to explain himself later.

She inquired at the desk. No, Mr. Hollister had not been in the lobby recently. At least no one had seen him. Had the lady checked his room?

"I will, thank you. Where is the ladies' room, please?"

"Ah, I think it's being cleaned."

"I will go up to my room."

"If you'll just wait one moment, madam. I'll check. I'm sure the crew is done cleaning."

The desk clerk came out from behind the desk and crossed the lobby.

Marianne drifted away from the desk, not really knowing what to do. She didn't want to waste time traipsing up to her room. Then again, Tom could be anywhere. But she thought she'd check around the ground floor first. He may even have gone outside. But why? She hadn't a clue. Something had happened, that she was sure.

But what should she do right now?

The desk clerk returned. "It's ready, madam. Right over there, next to the gift shop."

"Thank you very much."

First things first. She would answer the call of nature; then she would look for Tom.

She turned away from the desk, saw LAVATORY—LADIES, and made for the sign.

What a nice place! Reminded her of bathrooms in Europe. Some of the ones she'd seen in New York had been shocking. Utter squalor and filth. To say nothing of the smell.

This was wonderful. The marble was so pretty. She wondered what mountain it came from. Somewhere local, surely, she thought. It rivaled Italy's best.

The attendant was a blond German-looking woman. "Good evening, miss," she said, and opened the door to a stall. "This one I just cleaned."

"Thank you."

Here was *le commode,* inside the stall. Very nice. Yes, running water down there? No, it looked still. Very well.

She lifted her skirt and undid herself, which took some doing because what she wore underneath was elaborate. Then she sat. She noticed that the door was flush with the floor. She'd never seen that. Complete privacy. Good for hiding, if she ever had to duck in here in a chase. You couldn't simply stoop and look under the doors to see if there were any occupants. Bad for the gendarmes, actually. Well, the hotel was not built for the police, but for the guests, and if half of what she'd heard about San Francisco were true, this was a wide-open town. Practically run by *le demimonde.* Only thing, it was dark in here. The only light came through the stall's open top.

The lights went out.

Immediately upon the fall of darkness, there came a rumbling sound somewhere near. She looked around, could see nothing. The stall shook a little, and she thought: earthquake? What a time! Perhaps she should run outside? She had never experienced an earthquake before, and hoped mightily that the hotel's structure was up to it. Wouldn't do to have the building come down on her head.

The stall shook a bit more, and she decided to get up, having accomplished her purpose anyway. It was then that her eyes were able to make out her surroundings in the faint light that came from the entrance. She now saw that the door to the stall had risen.

No! The floor of the stall had sunk. She looked directly up. The ceiling of the ladies' room had either risen, or she and the stall were sinking into the floor.

To her surprise and chagrin, the latter was true.

She leaped up and tried to get a grip on the door handle, but missed and fell. Damned dress. Well, get rid of it.

She reached under the skirt and pulled two rip cords. Instantly, the bottom of her crinoline skirt fell away to reveal what she wore underneath. Not petticoats, but riding breeches and boots, a belt, a dagger in its scabbard.

The stall was now a shaft of polished travertine, smooth and slick, offering no purchase for climbing.

But there was a way up. Marianne raised her left boot and placed it against the wall to her back, putting pressure on it while bracing her upper body with her arms. The floor dropped away, and she raised the other foot and placed it against the shaft. Thus, she was suspended in air, watching the commode and the bottom of the stall drop away.

Now, all that remained was to "walk" up the shaft in this strange fashion, like a spider with four legs. On reaching the top of the stall, she would simply climb over and out.

Easier said than done, especially with the walls so smoothly polished. The top of the stall was a good five meters above her. But she rose slowly, taking a few steps at a time.

Her arms grew tired very quickly. And her boots, leather- soled, were slipping. The bottom of the shaft had sunk almost a story now, from what she could see in the darkness below. A fall now would be hurtful, if not injurious.

She struggled upward, sweat beading and running from her face. She had to stop halfway up and get her breath, but she quickly resumed the climb. She was almost level with the old floor now, and she gave some brief thought to how she might open the stall door without falling. It would be very difficult to unlatch while remaining braced one-handed. If there had been a half-door, *comme d'habitude*, it would have been easy to grab hold of the ledge. But there was no ledge. And trying to unlatch the door might simply send her dropping like a stone. No, no, she would have to climb all the way to the top.

Suddenly, light spilled into the bottom of the shaft. A door had opened down there. She heard men's voices. Someone came into the stall, a man with a balding head.

He scratched that head, then looked up and grinned wide. "Well, what do you know. Look at that, Turk."

Another man, thin and wiry, wedged himself into the stall and looked up. He had a face like a praying mantis.

"I'll be damned," Turk said. "She looks like a monkey. How do we get her down from there?"

"I dunno. Throw something."

Turk left the stall and returned momentarily with a length of rope.

"That ain't gonna do anything."

"Yes, it is. Tie this half a cinder block to the end of it, like this, see."

"Yeah, good. That'll do it. I'll get out. You throw it up."

Turk's first try to snare Marianne fell short. His second try, however, hooked her left leg, the block falling between her legs, scraping the back of her right knee in the process. It smarted.

This angered her. Turk yanked, and Marianne's left leg came off the wall. She nearly fell, but managed to shake off the line to let the block drop back down.

"Look out!"

Turk ducked out of the way.

"Goddamn it, nearly got brained. Just shoot her, for crissake."

"No, we got orders. We gotta climb up there."

"We can't climb up there, for crissake. Now, where the hell did that thing go?"

As Turk rooted behind the commode, Marianne decided this was the time to take the offensive. She dropped, coming down with her boots on the back of Turk's neck. His head went straight into the commode. Her fall well-broken, Marianne went sprawling out the bottom door into a basement space, where no fewer than four men pounced on her before she could get her knife out.

She became all fists and feet, her punches and kicks finding chests, bellies, heads, and groins.

As Marianne finally drew her knife, all four men retreated a few steps out in a circle, nursing injuries and picking up boards, some of which were wickedly nailed. Then, as if on signal, they all converged on her. She broke two boards and got in three vicious kicks and a good, solid punch before they tied her up.

"Get the knife, get the—ooof!"

"Vicious little vixen, ain't she?"

"Tigress . . . ow! . . . damn it, she bit me!"

"I got it!"

Turk, wet and slimy and his pride injured, staggered out of the stall, which in fact was a hydraulic elevator car. He saw the knot of men and one woman, whipped out a blackjack, waited for the woman's head to come around, and hit her with all his might. She went down and stayed down.

"Probably killed her," the balding man said.

"Don't give a damn if I did," Turk said.

Six

SIMULTANEOUSLY, TOM BROUGHT his right arm up between the knife and his neck and drove his left elbow into the ribs of the person behind him. Then he wrapped up his assailant's head in both his arms and levered the body over his shoulder. Whoever it was flew a couple of yards.

But to no ill effect; the smelly straw was apparently everywhere.

There came rustling and grunting.

"I wouldn't move if I were you," Tom said.

"Why?" came a voice.

"Because I have a derringer pointed right at you."

"OK. I'm not moving. But you can't really see me, can you?"

"No, but my ears are pretty good. Want to test them?"

"Let's make sure we're enemies, first. I'm John North, of the American Secret Service."

A click sounded as Tom engaged the pistol's safety mechanism. He sighed. "Tom Olam, Bavarian Secret Service."

"Olam! Finally we meet. Here, hope you can find my hand in the dark. Good to have you aboard."

"Uh, what am I aboard?"

"I don't quite know. We might be outside the hotel entirely, in a warren of underground tunnels and chambers. Tongs dug 'em out, I think."

"Tongs? Chinese gangs?"

"Right. They're old, maybe dating from the 1850s. Right above us, I think, is a stable across the alley from the hotel. They've been throwing old hay down here for years. Hell of a fire hazard. Should be cited. But the stuff broke my fall."

"And mine," Tom said. "How do we get out of here?"

"Well, if we had light to see, we could maybe see a way out. I got here without a lucifer, a flint, or anything. They searched me."

"They didn't me," Tom said. "I got chased in here by the Invisible Man."

"He's here, too? Egads. Every damned spook in the world came to this fish fry."

"Afraid they did. Probably more of them than we know. You never know the real masterminds. If they're any good, that is."

"The Master," North said.

"Yeah."

"We've been trying to ferret him out for years," North said. "We can't pin anything on him. But there've been some strange doings around the continent over the past few years. Mysterious stuff, and we don't have anyone concrete to blame. I'd give anything to know his hideout. We think it might be in northern California. So, when we heard of this convention, we made sure to have representatives here."

"Too bad about Jarvis."

"We don't even know where they hid his body. Could be in the bay."

Light blossomed in the gloom. Tom held up a burning lucifer. "Speaking of fire hazards," he said, "this isn't recommended, but we gotta see. Hey, is that a hole in the ceiling?"

North, a blue-jawed man with blue-black hair up in a sort of pompadour, shaded his eyes. "Wow, that's bright. Can't see, a little blinded."

"It's a hole, take my word for it. There're two, actually. One in the wall lower down, in this area. . . ."

"That's where we came sliding out."

"And one way up above."

"That's the hole they throw the hay through. It may lead up to the stable. I got no fancy gear on me. You got anything?"

"Yeah, may have."

The light went out. Tom knew his special equipment blindfolded. First he took off his coat and fished through it. Getting out a blank charge for the derringer, he loaded the gun with it, then rooted in a secret pocket of his coat for the spear piton. Finding it, he brought it out and inserted it into the barrel of the derringer. Then he brought out the end of a thin fishing line and threaded it through an eye in the piton. He tied the line off, then aimed the gun at the ceiling. Striking another lucifer with his free hand, he took aim at a spot on the rough rock wall near the small opening above. He fired.

The spear piton hit the ceiling just a foot or so to the right of the hole, piercing the soft limestone and sticking into it.

The lucifer faded, but not before North had observed and understood.

He said, "You have a Chalmers climber at the end of the that line, don't you?"

"You make the light," Tom said, handing over some lucifers.

North struck one and saw that the bottom end of the line did indeed attach to a thin cylinder with a spool in the middle of it. Tom gripped the cylinder with both hands and began to wring it. The gadget clicked and ratcheted, drawing in small increments of line and refusing to pay any back out. In this manner, it was possible to inch one's way up any sheer wall, as long as the strength of the climber held out.

Tom was about a quarter of the way up the wall when something fiery came shooting out of the lower opening.

"What's that?" Tom said.

"Someone threw a torch down the chute."

"Oh. At least we'll have light."

"At least. To say nothing of smoke and heat."

"Better hurry."

It was hard to hurry with one's full weight on the line. One could only wrench and ratchet, wrench and ratchet, going up bit by tiny bit. At first, Tom relieved his weight a little by finding purchase with his cleated boots against the cavern's wall. But the wall sloped away, and he was dangling free.

Flames spread quickly through the dry straw. In no time, the cavern filled with smoke.

Below and in the midst of the conflagration, North choked and coughed. Tom fared no better, for the smoke was billowing upward.

At last, Tom reached the hole, stuck his arm in to find a handhold, found one, and dangled in space. After he depressed a button on the spool, the Chalmers climber began to pay out line and dropped.

"Climber coming down!" Tom yelled. "You OK?"

"Yeah!"

Tom struggled to get up into the narrow tunnel, in reality a fissure between two masses of rock, which would be easy to climb. Faint light spilled from above. An exit, Tom hoped.

But first, North had to ratchet his way out of the cavern before getting roasted. There was nothing for Tom to do. After assuring himself that North was on his way up, he began to explore the fissure, climbing up its length about five feet, where he discovered that the passage widened out into a small chamber.

Filled with rats.

Little eyes glowed in the dark, hundreds of them. A nest, he'd stumbled into a rats' nest.

Yuck.

The eyes moved forward, and soft, furry things began to nuzzle up to him. He batted them away, but more came at him, squeaking and sniffing. Tiny cold, wet noses laved and prodded.

He ducked back down the tube and saw that North was halfway up, but flames were licking at his heels.

"North! Hurry up!"

"Doing my best!"

Tom reached for the line. He'd have to try to pull the man up. The fishing line dug deeply into his palms, but he ignored the pain and pulled as smoke stung his eyes and superheated fumes seared his nose.

A rat landed on his head. He ignored that, too, but it was hard to remain blasé about the thing as it climbed down his head to his neck, where it began to nuzzle and nibble his right ear.

"You dirty rat," Tom said through clenched teeth.

He gave his head a few shakes, but the creature held on. He shook again, but the little critter tenaciously clung, its tiny claws digging into Tom's flesh.

Below, North was still ratcheting slowly. The fire had abated a little, stunted by the dwindling oxygen. But now breathing was another problem, and by the time North was within Tom's reach, both men were on the verge of passing out. When Tom finally grabbed him and hauled him up, North was only partly conscious, so Tom had to drag him up though the tunnel while fighting off panicked rats and getting pelted by falling rubble, along with the odd rat dropping or two.

Up and up, the damned shaft seemed to have no top. A good five yards up, North revived enough to climb himself, which helped the situation immensely. The men scrabbled up the hole. Mercifully, most of the rats had preceded them. Back in the chamber, the flames had just about snuffed out, but the smoke was now as thick as steam, venting up through the shaft.

It was like crawling up a chimney with a fire in the grate. Tom's seared eyes could only pick out daylight above. He struggled upward, barely hanging on to consciousness. The next thing he knew, he was out of the hole, sprawled on a straw-covered dirt floor, hacking and wheezing. When he caught his breath, he sat up and saw that North had made it out of the hole, but in considerably worse shape. Blackened face contorted in pain, he was having some real difficulty breathing.

North croaked. "Chest hurts like hell."

"Smoke inhalation. You need fresh air. Can you walk?"

"I think."

Tom helped him up, and they both staggered out of a junk-filled back room into the stable proper, where two stableboys greeted their arrival with some surprise.

"Where the blazes you two come from?" one of them asked.

"That's about the size of it," Tom said in passing.

Seven

TOM WAS PUTTING the finishing touches on his new disguise when John North, cleaned up and almost completely recovered, stepped back into the hotel room.

Different hotel room, different hotel entirely: the Empire Hotel, just down the street from the Palace. It wasn't much of a hotel, but it was clean and, so far as Tom could tell, free of booby traps and man traps.

"You look the picture of Dr. Richard Owen, dinosaur hunter," North said.

"Nice suit," Tom said. "Going pretty much as myself. I've never seen a picture of Owen, come to think of it."

"His face isn't all that well-known. The dinosaurs he discovered are, but not their discoverer."

"Which is good, if I'm to impersonate him. Let's just hope he doesn't show up."

"He won't," North said. "But there's a reservation in his name at the Palace. We made it. Don't worry, Tom, Owen isn't a public figure in the states. You won't be recognized."

"Still, I'm going to need luck."

"What about me? I'm going as Dr. Lovelorn. He's a dwarf, but few people know it."

"Aren't you worried about what the underworld might know?"

"Our informers tell us that almost nothing is known about Lovelorn, and we've been back-leaking false information for months in preparation for this masquerade. I'm going to be on fairly solid ground impersonating him. I just hope he hasn't broken out of federal prison again."

"At least we're pretty sure Lovelorn isn't masterminding this plot," Tom said. "What are your guesses as to who is?"

North lifted his shoulders. "At a convention of masterminds, who can tell?"

"The Invisible Man?"

"Well, he's a wild card. But maybe he's the kingpin."

"Maybe. Little is known about his capabilities."

Tom shook his head. "Things have been mighty strange ever since I arrived in this town."

"Things have been fairly strange in this entire region recently."

"Really? How so?"

"We've been getting odd reports from our intelligence sources all over northern California. Sightings of strange, unidentified flying craft in the Mount Shasta area, for one."

"Mount Shasta? A base for Robur?"

"We don't think so," North said. "Also, stuff even more fantastic. People reporting that close relatives, friends, neighbors are not who they seem to be. They're changed, different. Right out of fairy stories."

"Changelings," Tom said. "Interesting."

"Some form of communicable hysteria, probably."

"Hope so," Tom said. "Listen, it's almost nine-thirty. Marianne will be frantic. See you back at the hotel?"

"Get going. And feel free to consider this room a redoubt if you get into trouble over there. See you at the big conspiracy meeting, or whatever it is. Ten o'clock."

"Thanks. Appreciate the cooperation."

North took Tom's hand and shook it warmly. "Thanks for saving my life. I wouldn't have gotten out of that cavern if it weren't for you."

"Think nothing of it. Listen, sorry about Jarvis getting it. I wish I could have understood what he was trying to say."

"What's your guess?" North asked.

"Well, it started with 'auto,' but he couldn't get the rest out."

North rubbed his chin. "Automotive, automatic, auto . . ."

"Automobile?"

"What's an automobile?"

"Uh, nothing."

"Straighten your cravat. Here, let me."

"Thanks. See you later."

BY THE TIME Tom had arrived yet again at the Palace and checked into yet anther hotel room, it was his turn to be frantic, for Marianne was not in her room and nowhere in sight.

Of course, the desk knew nothing. Neither did the bell captain, the housekeeper, or any of the bellboys. Tom didn't bother to inform Quintus.

Maybe she would show up at the conspiracy meeting. Tom checked the clock in the lobby. Almost ten. OK, penthouse. He'd always wanted to party in a penthouse. Ask the elevator guy.

It was a different elevator guy. High employee turnover in this place. Well, it was the night shift. He'd like to have a little talk with the joker who'd taken him to the basement.

Wait a minute. Was that going to happen again?

Probably not. His new room was fine, no booby traps. No one could possibly know that he was here as Richard Owen, for he'd decided to impersonate the man less than an hour ago. So, until someone penetrated the ruse, he was safe—that is, unless someone had it in for Owen. Highly improbable, but you never knew. He had briefly thought of coming to the convention as John Carter of Mars, in this universe a real person.

In this universe, fact is fiction, fiction is fact, Tom thought as he rode the elevator up to the twelfth floor. Also, possibility was actuality, as was, sometimes, improbability.

Sometimes the Falkenstein universe got a little hairy.

"Twelfth floor, penthouse, Emperor's Suite."

Case in point. An "emperor" did live up here. The emperor of California, in fact. Most everyone in California recognized Joshua Abraham Norton as "Norton I, Emperor of California and Protector of Mexico." He had existed in the history that Tom knew, but had been viewed as a madman. Here, he still had wide, popular support after the cabal of landed interests, whose pawn he had been, had been smashed.

But what about now? Who was running this show? Here were Slocum and his buddy Jean-Claude, among other goons, checking guests' invitations, frisking people. Did Moriarty or whoever stage a coup in California? Or did the emperor himself extend this hospitality? If so, was he a crook, too?

Hard to tell.

"Invitation, sir?" Jean-Claude seemed uncharacteristically friendly.

"Yes, indeed," Tom said, handing it over.

"Yes, sir. Right inside, sir, through double doors."

Old Jean-Claude seemed oblivious, no recognition at all. Tom had tussled with him directly. There was Slocum. Look him directly in the eyes, just to test? Better not. No use asking for it. He's looking the other way.

Good. The disguise was working. Clean-shaven with longish blond hair, Tom may not have looked anything like Owen, but he most certainly did not resemble Jake Hollister.

Still, some people could pick out a face. It would do well to keep to the sidelines.

Inside was a suite tastefully decorated in the Spanish Colonial style—dark, oiled wood against white stucco walls—with a wine and cheese party in full swing. Local product. Tom sampled a dry red, then a semisweet white. Good, very good. But while he sipped and munched (cheese, also good), he was looking desperately around for Marianne. She should be working a room like this.

There was Lord Yosho Tomino, in silk kimono and sandals, samurai swords (long and short) sticking out wickedly.

Here was Adam von Richten, Prussian inventor of the lunar shell and the "ether protective garment." A space suit.

Over there, in the corner, talking with two Berlin underworld figures, stood Alvin Dumont, French inventor of the steam uniped.

Oh, and Adolf von Shrakenberg, Prussian Landfortress designer. He was having the blush, along with a bit of the sharp cheddar.

And there was Rhyme Enginemaster, the dwarf engineer of Castle Falkenstein, royal engineer to the court of His Majesty, Ludwig II, King of Bayern.

Rhyme stared right through Tom, as he should have. As planned.

Good boy. Oops. Stout fellow.

The room was stuffed wall to wall with technological geniuses, all eccentric, all a bit of the megalomaniac, even the ones essentially benign.

OK, what was the strategy here? To recruit the best and most inventive scientific minds into a world

criminal organization? To wheedle and cajole them?
To threaten them? Not that last, probably, because
wine and cheese aren't the usual way to do it. But
what was the draw, here? What kind of snake oil was
going to be pitched?

Who were the pitchmen? Here and there among
the geniuses, chatting them up, were a few notorious organized crime figures from around the world.
Tom recognized them all from Secret Service file photos. Were they even now pitching the "World Science League" as an alliance of scientist and criminal?

Where the *hell* was Marianne? Now he was
beginning to get good and worried.

"Gentlemen—and what ladies there are—may I
have your attention?"

All turned to Jules Verne, who stood by the
immensely long sofa.

"Thank you one and all for attending this affair,
and this first convention of the World Science
League. I am not your host. The person who is your
host—rather, hostess— will be talking to you
presently, but I would like to extend my thanks and
appreciation to all concerned who had a hand in this
singular affair. It is a unique opportunity for men—
and ladies—on the frontier of science to meet, con-
verse, and otherwise hobnob. A rare occasion.
Without further ado, then, may I present our host-

ess, one of the best minds of the century, for all that it is a female mind—the Lady Ada Lovelace!"

Tom nearly dropped his wineglass. But the woman who walked out of a dark corner was not Marianne impersonating Ada Lovelace.

It was Ada Lovelace herself.

"Olam."

The voice came at his back. He dared not turn.

"Olam, I must speak to you."

Tom swiveled his head slowly around, putting on his best innocent expression.

It was a tall, bald man with a monocle and a handlebar mustache. Though the features were faintly familiar, Tom did not recognize the man.

"Uh, were you speaking to me, sir?"

"Yes," the man said in a rumbling whisper. "I know who you are. If you wish to avoid being exposed here and now, you will accompany me through that door into the next room, for a private talk."

Tom nodded pleasantly, as if agreeing to a game of billiards.

"Be happy to, later, but I want to hear what the lady says."

"She is going to tell everyone that an international organization of scientists can lead the world into an epoch of sanity, prosperity, and peace. It is pure balderdash. The real purpose of this gathering will not be alluded to. Only I know the real purpose. At least in part."

Tom listened for a few moments. Lady Lovelace was indeed launching into a spiel along the lines of the one the man had just outlined.

"OK, let's go."

They threaded their way through the crowd, Tom leading.

Once in the next room, after shutting the door, the man drew close to Tom and looked him straight in the eyes.

"I know you, sir. Do you know me? Look closely."

Tom peered into dark eyes. He took a step back and considered them in the stern, stony face before him. Recognition dawned. He took two more steps back.

"Moriarty."

"The same. Very good, Mr. Olam. You seem to feel that I bear you some animosity, and you want to keep your distance. You are quite correct. I do not forget easily our last meeting, when you were so kind as to throw a bomb into my skiff, down in the sewers of Paris."

"That was regrettable," Tom said. "But I felt I had to make a statement."

"Very droll. However, I am willing to call a truce. We have now a common enemy to fight. I am going to admit to you something that I have admitted to no man before. I need your help."

Tom let out a burst of laughter. "You need *my* help?"

"Please be quiet. Yes. It is unbearably embarrassing. But I must now admit that I am allied with forces that threaten to overwhelm me."

"What is it, Moriarty? Literally in league with the devil this time?"

Moriarty considered it seriously. "It very well could be. It is some force which I cannot quite fathom."

"What have you done with the Countess Marianne?"

"I have done nothing with her."

"Your goons abducted Verne. They are working as doormen at this party."

"They abducted Dr. Verne, carrying out a preconceived plan of which I was a part. This is quite true. And it is also true that an impostor was to be put in his place. We employed a professional actor for the purpose. But that actor is nowhere to be found, and the thing out there that calls itself Verne suddenly appeared. I then realized that the forces I am in league with had designs of their own. Those two goons, as you call them, are no longer my employees."

"You're saying Verne and your men are. . . ."

"Duplicates. Simulacra. They are clockwork simulacra of a type so advanced that it surpasses understanding."

Tom was silent, his mind working furiously. He was weighing everything Moriarty had said, picking it apart, testing, doubting. Moriarty was a consummate liar. But this . . . Tom did not know what to make of it.

"How do you know they aren't simply drugged?"

"I do not think so. Haven't you noticed something strange about many employees of this hotel?"

"Now that you mention it, yes. They're also clockwork?"

"Perhaps. Perhaps they are not duplicates of anybody in particular. I think it is likely that they are in most cases. In any event, Mr. Olam, they are not human."

"Oh, come now, Moriarty."

Moriarty's dark brows drew together. "Jules Verne disappeared, did he not?"

"Yes."

"And when you next saw him, was something different about him?"

Reluctantly, Tom had to admit that Moriarty had something. He had to face the fact that this wild theory explained a lot. "Yes. Something strange."

Tom walked off and stared out the window. The city was a sparkling web of lights spun up and down many hills.

"The Verne that reappeared is an automaton," Moriarty said.

"Automaton! I'll be damned. So that's what Jarvis Gresham was trying to say."

"Who?"

"The American Secret Service agent your 'employees' killed."

"He must have divined that something was going on."

"But your goons killed him, and before they were supposedly duplicated."

"That was a mistake. Jean-Claude LeBec is—was—a congenital idiot, and demented to boot. For that blunder I would have eliminated him, eventually."

Tom turned from the window. "Inhuman. Are you saying these duplicates are alien beings? From some other planet?" Taking a stab in the dark, Tom was thinking of the "unidentified aircraft" seen near Mount Shasta.

Moriarty shrugged. "The exact nature of the entity behind this conspiracy is mysterious. However, I do know that even as we speak, people attending this convention are being abducted."

"I can attest to that. But you don't know the purpose?"

"No, not as yet. Though what we have here is something entirely new, entirely unprecedented. It is a plot, sir. A plot against everyone, including the plotters of the world, of whom I am chief. This particular ploy is also directed against the world's best scientists. Some of them, perhaps all who attend, will sometime this weekend be abducted, and possibly doppelgängered. Duplicated. And the duplicate put in the original's place."

"What is done with the originals? What happened to the real Verne?"

"That I do not know. As I said, I have just stumbled onto the fact that more is going on here that I knew of previously."

"Who, Moriarty? Who is it that you're in league with? The Master?"

"No. I have been communicating with an entity named Primus. Though I have only been in direct contact with its agents."

"Its?"

"Its."

The door opened, and Jean-Claude stuck his head in. He smiled. "Messieurs, you are missing the talk."

"We are having a private conversation," Moriarty said.

"I see. But you are rude, monsieur."

"Damn you. . . ."

"I think we'd better step back in," Tom said diplomatically. He had no idea what was going on, but he wanted to get to the bottom of the mystery of Ada Lovelace's appearance here, and that might be better accomplished by listening to her firsthand.

"We'd best continue this conversation later," Tom said to Moriarty.

"As you wish. Meet me in the lobby after the meeting."

The proceedings in the main room had shifted to the question-and-answer segment. As Tom walked in, Lord Tomino was speaking.

"—but how do we divide the world up into spheres of influence? Who will arbitrate this process?"

"There will be a judiciary system in the new order to handle disputes," Lady Lovelace answered, "as there was in the old order."

"Then what is the difference, Lady?"

"The difference is that reason and rationality will rule, not primitive animal emotion, prejudice, and superstition."

"Ah, but one man's superstition is another's rationality."

Tom was studying Lady Lovelace, and came to a stunning realization.

This was not the original.

Could Moriarty's paranoid ramblings be truth? All the facts seemed to be adding up to that conclusion.

Wait a minute. Primus. Quintus. Sextus.

Egads, Tom thought, sitting down. No, it was just too fantastic. Things like alien invasion did not happen in the universe of Castle Falkenstein, one out of an infinite number of universes accessible by the Faerie Veil's magic doorway. Universes came in flavors. The flavor of Castle Falkenstein (or, rather, the flavor of the universe in which Castle Falkenstein, King Ludwig's lavish fortress, was reality rather than royal daydream) was a rich, red-velvet Victorian. Nothing like alien space beings had ever cropped up in it, nor were they likely to. They just didn't belong here, and Tom couldn't believe Moriarty's conspiracy theories. Other universes, Tom had been assured by faerie folk who knew, were very high-tech, and featured ray guns, interstellar travel, and other wonders. But not old Falkenstein, the universe of sabers, steam tech, and pepperbox pistols. True, in the Falkenstein universe the nineteenth century always threatened to become the twentieth ahead of schedule, if certain other nasty faerie folk, namely the Unseelie, had their way. But Tom's mission (if he chose to accept it, and he most certainly did) was to see to it that the twentieth century arrived not one second before it absolutely had to.

"This is preposterous," Richard von Ruppelt shouted. "Are you seriously proposing that we here in this room supplant the existing governments of the world by violently overthrowing them?"

"What's preposterous about that?" said an Oriental man who Tom recognized as the leading gang leader in . . . what was it, Saigon or Singapore? "I think it is an excellent idea. Why, here in this room are the creators of almost every fantastic weapon of science in the world. Surely taking power by violence will be no problem in principle."

"Not by violence, surely," Verne countered. "That won't be necessary. There is more than enough intelligence in this room to secure the necessary power by other means. As to the moral justification of this undertaking, it isn't as if the existing governments are doing a first-rate job. An idiot could do better."

"Verne, I'm surprised at you," von Ruppelt said. "I wouldn't have expected you to be a party to this nonsense."

"It's not governments that we must improve," Victor Frankenstein said. "It's man himself."

"Hear, hear," came agreement around the room.

"The human being is a sorry creature," Frankenstein went on. "Barely a step up from the ape. But as scientists, we have it in our power to improve him greatly. We can raise his status from that of a hairless ape to that of a god!"

"Possible," Lady Lovelace said. "Very possible, in the future."

"It is possible now!" Frankenstein insisted.

"You are more right than you know, Frankenstein. But first a rule of reason and sanity must be established. Only then can scientific progress flourish."

"The lady may be right," Frankenstein conceded.

"Heaven knows my own work has been stifled by the pettiness of small, obtuse minds." His mouth curled bitterly.

"Baron Frankenstein, in the coming era of World Science," Lady Lovelace said, "you will be free to conduct your research in an atmosphere of encouragement and support."

"Thank Heaven for that."

The discussion continued as the room bifurcated into those who favored a revolutionary approach to a scientists' takeover and those who thought gradualism the more prudent course of action. In time, those few attendees categorically opposed to the whole idea in principle found themselves a marginalized minority, and Tom could have rattled off its roster days before. The only names missing now were Verne's and Lovelace's. But were these the real Verne and Lovelace?

The meeting dragged on without any further significant developments. All agreed to disagree, and this gave Tom some comfort. He could not believe that a group composed almost exclusively of mavericks, misfits, and megalomaniacs could ever come to any agreement, general or specific.

So, that was that. The convention, the program, the upshot. And the rest was mummery.

And as to Moriarty's fanciful musings—well, obviously he'd had a falling out with some of the organizers, and was trying to muddy the waters as much as he could. What his plan was, Tom would not hazard a guess. But this was not unusual; Moriarty's plans and intentions were always obscure, to say the least.

The only thing he wanted to do now was to talk with Lady Lovelace. Tom could not fathom her at all. He wanted to know where she'd been for the past several months, and why she'd shown up here as one of the ringleaders of "World Science."

Did she owe Tom an explanation? Not particularly, but Tom was determined to get some semblance of a story out of her.

"Lady Lovelace. . . ."

But she and Verne disappeared behind the big sliding doors from which she'd made her grand entrance. Slocum blocked the way.

"I'd like to talk with the lady and Dr. Verne," Tom told him.

Slocum stiff-armed him. "No chance."

"This is getting to be a nasty habit with you," Tom said.

"I never seen you before tonight, Mister."

"I don't take lightly to being shoved around."

"Sorry, sir, she and him doesn't want to be disturbed. This is a private suite, you know. Look, everyone is leaving. Probably going down to the bar for liquor and cigars. You oughta join 'em."

"Later. I must see Lady Lovelace."

"Can't do that, sir."

"Is this gentleman giving you trouble, Jeem?"

Tom brushed Jean-Claude's hand from his shoulder and shoved him away. "Open the door."

"Look, we don't want to have to get rough with you. . . ."

Tom's right fist connected with Slocum's gut.

Slocum smiled.

"Ahhhh!" Tom let out a yell, and was very puzzled, not to mention pained. It had been like slamming his fist into a cement-filled punching bag. His hand throbbed.

Jean-Claude rammed into Tom and sent him crashing into the doors. He ricocheted back, wobbling on his feet, and Jean-Claude followed up with a right smash that sent him down. Consciousness ebbing away, Tom struggled to get up, and succeeded, only to have Slocum award him a stunning wallop across the face.

For the next few minutes the two thugs threw Tom around the room, and Tom had little to say in the matter. His every punch bounced ineffectually off adamantine flesh; landing a kick was like fetching a foot up against a stone wall. His judo holds failed or were countermanded. The thugs laughed off chairs smashed over their heads. They batted away things thrown at them: vases, candlesticks, ashtrays, and a ten-pound chunk of Sierra quartz shot through with threads of gold.

Presently, the two thugs got around to picking Tom up off the floor. They dusted him off; then they threw him at an eight-foot-tall glass-fronted high-boy full of Indian pottery.

When all the crashing and tinkling stopped, Tom lifted his head out of the shards of crystal and crockery and raised one finger to say weakly, "On second thought, I'll stop back later."

"C'mon, Jean-Claude," Slocum said, "let's throw this garbage down the chute."

Tom was hurting so much, he just let them do it. They picked up as though he were a bag of trash and dragged him into a kitchen. Then they stuffed him into a dumbwaiter.

"Next stop, basement," Slocum announced as the miniature elevator descended.

Tom rode down into darkness.

Eight

RAYS OF LIGHT like bright spears lanced out of the darkness.

There was no sound but an incessant clicking.

Marianne stood in the darkness, dressed in only her shift, fingers of light playing over her lithe body. Other fingers held her, but not human ones. Metal ones, cold, unfeeling. They held her lightly, with only enough pressure to keep her standing erect. She wobbled a little, but was able to stand.

She didn't want to stand. She wanted to lie down again and rest. Her head throbbed. The pain was like a great weight pressing down on the top of her head. She wanted to sleep again so she wouldn't have to hear the clicking and clattering, which hadn't stopped since she had awakened. She didn't know where this place was or what it was, but she thought it might be Hell. Pain, darkness, fear. That's all there was here. But what was the light? The needles of light that stabbed her eyes. She couldn't understand that. Hell had no light, just eternal darkness.

Or was this the Darkness Visible? She remembered the phrase, but couldn't think of the source . . . what was the name? Oh.

She couldn't think.

The play of light over her body stopped, and the shadows reclaimed her, the metal arms dragging her back down, arranging her limbs, strapping her down.

She was borne away on invisible wheels, trundling off into the darkness. Sleep began to drag her into oblivion.

No!

Don't sleep. Sleep is death. Stay awake.

She forced her eyes open, searched the shadows for something, anything recognizable. Shapes came and went. Wheels? Gears? Ropes, pulleys? Mechanical stuff. She was being borne through the belly of a great mechanical beast whose call was the clatter and clink and click of joints and armatures and relays and eccentric linkages.

But that made no sense. This couldn't be.

But it was. She dismissed all attempts at an explanation. One thing was paramount: she must escape.

There was nothing holding her now, nothing but a strap.

However, it was a tight strap.

She had been stripped of most of her clothing, but not of all the clever gadgets and aids hidden in secret pockets in that clothing. She still had a few tricks in reserve. She moved one hand to the hem of her shift and carefully slipped a tiny blade out of a secret and almost invisible pocket. The blade was razor sharp.

Something glinted in the shadows ahead. A mote of reflected light, or refracted light, in glass? Yes, glass, a glass tube, out of which protruded a wicked needle.

She cut the straps, rolled off the conveyor belt, and hit the stone floor hard. Above her, the needle jabbed at air.

A few minutes later, she had crawled a few feet over the cold floor, but she had no idea where she was going. Inches above her head, flywheels spun, belts flapped, gears meshed. Cautiously, slowly, she kept crawling in one direction until she was convinced she was simply getting deeper into the machinery. So she pivoted on her stomach and went the opposite way, inching back over the same dangerous territory, metal teeth snapping and gnashing just above her face.

Finally, she passed out of the realm of machinery into a strange world populated by . . . she looked up.

Manikins? Department store dummies? Clothes horses?

She looked again.

Manikins, yes. But they looked entirely real. Like real people lined up in ranks and files, an army of statues ready to march.

She crept through a forest of legs, occasionally passing a severed arm or leg lying on the floor. She examined these. Inside the limbs were wheels and cables.

Automatons. She was crawling through a stockpile of automatons. Mechanical simulacra.

She crept on. Soon the ranks and files thinned out, and she came to a thicket of levers and control rods, which she skirted. She crawled through more darkness, then under a conveyor belt, then through another mechanical forest, this one of whirling lathes and drills and die cutters. Coming out into the open again, she saw bodies hanging in the gloom above, being conveyed by moving wires. A belt rolled just below, and on it sat armless half-bodies—heads, necks, shoulders, and trunks. Curious, she risked rising to a crouch. The torsos retreated off to the left. Another approached. She waited, wanting to examine it close up.

It came out of the gloom into faint light, and her breath left her lungs.

The face was hers. Her face.

She wanted to scream, but did not. Blindly, she groped her way back into the safety of the darkness, finally reaching a stone wall, along which she tread carefully.

She came to what looked like doors to a freight elevator. Carefully, she pushed them apart and confronted an empty shaft. The bottom of the shaft was only a few feet below the edge of the floor. A ladder ran up the side of the shaft, and this she began to climb.

Climbing was not difficult, but the task of getting out of the shaft did not appear easy. There were no access doors, and no way to reach the outer elevator doors from the ladder. She would have to climb to the roof.

Well, she would, if the elevator didn't come down on top of her. She flattened herself against the ladder. The elevator whistled by inches from her back, but passed without incident.

Letting out a sigh, she resumed climbing. After six floors, she weakened and had to rest. She took a minute, then continued.

At the very top of the ladder was a trap door leading to yet another room full of machinery, but this time just the huge pulley wheels of the elevator itself, turning and turning and drawing cable up through the floor and feeding it back down again.

Hanging on a hook by a door was a pair of grease-covered overalls, which she slipped into. They were filthy, but as it would be decidedly awkward to go parading around the hotel in her shift, they would do.

She cracked the door open and saw that this room full of cable wheels was actually a shed on the roof of a building. The hotel?

She checked both directions, then stepped out the door. Then she stole around the shed, on the look-out for anyone else on the roof with her. When she was sure she was alone, she looked down the side of the building and saw the top of the Palace's ornate facade. Looking out, she took in the view. Here she was, on the roof of one of the highest buildings in the city. From this side, she could see the lights of almost all the northern parts of the city, from the Embarcadero to Fort Point. Her head still throbbed, but the salt wind off the water refreshed her, gave her new life.

The sky was dark and starless. How long had she been unconscious down in that hellish cellar? Her memory of time was a blur.

She saw a smaller shed with another door in it, and she found this to be a stairway leading down into the building. Up from Hell to Heaven, and now down again.

She descended back into the world.

Nine

AT LEAST HE had time now, Tom thought as the dumbwaiter carried him down. Time to prepare, no one hitting him now.

Hard to think while two robots are working you over. He moved stiffly, muscles throbbing painfully, getting things out of his pockets, things to help.

The dumbwaiter continued to descend. No way to stop it from inside. The dumbwaiter transported dumb things up and down. He was a dumb thing. Dumb to have tackled those two gorillas up there.

But those two weren't gorillas. They weren't human, either. Nothing human could be that hard. There was metal under their latex skins, and under the metal, gears, cables, wheels, and bolts. No flesh, no blood, nothing warm and squishy.

Down and down. He wondered if any of his ribs had cracked. If so, he'd be good for nothing the rest of the weekend.

What are you complaining about? he thought. *They could easily have killed you.*

Down and still down. How many floors to the kitchen? Or was it to the kitchen he was going? He berated himself for not counting floors as the little doors went past. Try to knock one open? But the little car was descending too fast. No, he'd have to ride it to the bottom, however far down that was.

He was ready for the moment the door opened.

The dumbwaiter thumped to a halt. Voices outside. He heard the name "Turk" called.

The door opened, and a blade-faced man peered in with bulging, insect-like eyes. Not an alien, just plain ugly. Tom let a concussion grenade roll out. It dropped to the floor and bounced.

The man didn't take notice. "Here's another one—"

The grenade went off with a flash and a bang and a big puff of smoke. In the ensuing confusion, Tom wriggled out of the car. He hit a hard concrete floor, rolled, and came up swinging at two men who were standing there rubbing their eyes. He clouted one alongside the head and kicked the other's kneecap.

No metal this time. He connected with flesh and brittle bone. The two men went down.

Another came at him out of shadow, and Tom went at him with both feet in a flying kick. His boots slammed into a very human chest. The owner gasped and staggered back into a hollow.

Stairs. He dashed up a flight, took the landing in a bound, and ran up another flight, thumping through the door at its top.

He came out into the hotel's kitchen; it was dark and deserted. He passed through, sprinted the length of the darkened dining room, and ducked through a busboys' station to find himself in the hotel's bar.

"Ah, Mr. Olam."

Moriarty, seated in a booth toward the rear, beckoned.

"Sit down, please."

Tom walked over to the booth and sat. "I need a drink," he said.

"You look a little worse for wear," Moriarty commented. "Did you have trouble upstairs?"

"None I couldn't handle." Then a sharp pain laced up his side, and he winced.

"I see," Moriarty said dryly.

"Never mind. Tell me about Primus."

"As I said, I know almost nothing about Primus. I can only guess at its nature."

"You keep referring to Primus as an object."

"Not an inanimate one, I assure you."

"Why have we never heard of the thing? I'm trying to believe you, Moriarty. I do believe that there are automatons around here. I just had a tussle with two of them. But how can you credibly dissociate yourself from them?"

"I admitted to having a hand in planning this affair. You were meant to be drawn here, as well. The decoys were well-planted. You and your colleagues all over the globe took the bait. Secret agents, spies, secret police. And now you are targets, as well. But you are not my targets."

"Bosh. Are you still saying the World Crime League isn't behind this charade?"

"I am saying, Mr. Olam, that the World Crime League, of which I am the chief executive officer, is also a target. They—and I use the conspiratorial *they*—want to duplicate the leading underworld figures along with everyone else. Can't you see, Olam? This is the ultimate conspiracy. The conspiracy of conspiracies. It is a plot against the human race itself. It is monstrousness on a level . . . on such a scale. . . . "What, that you can only admire?"

Moriarty's smile looked as though it were the first in his life, bidding fair to crack his granite face. "I suppose."

"But who? Who's behind it all?"

"I will tell you what I know, through a long string of deduction and conjecture. The Lady Ada Lovelace has something to do with the mystery. It centers on her, and the cult of the Temple of Ra."

"What could the Ra cult have to do with it?"

"They have been experimenting, as you must know, with infusing sorcery into science."

"So's everybody in this crazy world. So what?"

"They have succeeded, I think, in creating a true form of artificial intelligence. A thinking machine. And I believe this conspiracy is the unwitting result. I think something went wrong."

"All this mummery is a Ra plot? Doesn't track, Moriarty. It just doesn't track. I'd like to hear what Lady Lovelace has to say about it."

"That was not Lady Lovelace, up in the penthouse. Did you get a good look at her?"

Tom nodded. Then he said, "I see."

"I think you do."

"Why are you here, Moriarty? And why in disguise?"

"I shall tell you. I got wind of a double cross long before this convention. I decided to go through the motions anyway, just to see what was going on. When I arrived in San Francisco, I noticed something strange. This hotel isn't the only establishment with automatons on the loose. The city is filled with them. They are in the government, in businesses, in shops, in factories. They are everywhere, and they are taking over."

Tom countered, "I just ran into some human thugs down in the basement."

"I did not say the automatons had completely taken over. You obviously had a dustup with those of the Crime League's minions who have not yet been automatized."

"Moriarty, what you've said so far makes very little sense. On the one hand, you organized this so-called convention. Now you say somebody else is behind it."

"You will remember that I had a most embarrassing admission. That admission was that I was outsmarted. Worse, I was tardy in realizing I was in league with an intelligence that far outstrips my own. Never before has this been true. I have lived my mental life in loneliness, despairing of ever meeting a mind the equal of mine. Now I have found one greater. And I do not like it, sir. I do not like it."

"How did you come in contact with this Primus?"

"Through a series of go-betweens whom I now realize were automatons. I conjectured that their puppeteer was the legendary Master. Not so, or Primus is indeed the Master. In any event, Primus proposed an alliance. Through many ways Primus made clear to me that his—I shall use the male pronoun for convenience—his resources were vast and powerful, and his base of operations was on another continent—here. I saw a chance to widen the scope of my enterprise, and agreed to collaborate. The plan was to throw a convention like this for scientists, and seek pledges of cooperation in a worldwide coup d'etat that would set up a provisional world government. Among the scientists, those whose cooperation we could not gain by persuasion we were to coerce by blackmail or extortion. World Crime was to take care of that end of it. We expected most of the major masterminds to throw in with us. The pure inventor types we were, of course, not sure of."

"When did you stumble onto all this, Moriarty? When did you know?"

"When Primus sent my own men to abduct me. They failed, and I fled to another hotel. I returned in disguise, and under a persona I had created for the contingency, complete with invitation."

Tom crossed his arms. "If this is a lie, it's the most elaborate one in history. What do you propose we do, Moriarty?"

"We must find Primus's base of operations."

"But what *is* Primus?" Tom asked pointedly.

Moriarty looked off into the distance. "A mind. A mind vast and labyrinthian. Pure mind, I think."

"Is it something otherworldly?"

"I do not know."

"Is it supernatural?"

"I suspect so."

"Where does it come from?"

"That I do not know either."

Tom sighed. "I need a drink."

"Let me order you one."

"Beer, please."

When a waiter brought Tom's beer, Tom looked him over. Human, he thought.

"The hotel staff is still part human."

"Probably mostly human," Moriarty said. "Only the management and a few strategic personnel have been replaced by automatons."

"But hasn't anybody noticed anything strange?"

"Perhaps. But if you were a chamber maid, would you run to the police with some wild story about the concierge having been replaced by a clockwork dummy?"

Tom nodded. "I see what you mean. But there have been stories of changelings circulating. Or so I've heard."

"As you've now seen for yourself, these stories are not mere folklore. But no one can prove a thing. Besides, the local constabulary have probably been deeply compromised already. There is nobody to tell any wild stories to."

"How about the Emperor Norton?"

"Oh, very likely duplicated long ago," Moriarty said. "After all, he lives in this hotel."

"Where is he now? Or his dummy."

"South, mending fences with the hacienda *caudillos*. And probably acting on the instructions of Primus."

"Well, he probably—" Tom's jaw sagged.

Moriarty's head turned. "Eh, what is it?"

Marianne came strolling into the bar wearing baggy overalls with straps that barely covered strategic areas. Eyeballs clicked the length and breadth of the place.

"Good Lord." Tom got to his feet, shed his coat, wrapped Marianne up in it, then let her slide into the booth. Moriarty rose and solemnly bowed. "Good evening, Countess,"

Moriarty said.

Marianne recognized him and froze. She gave Tom a puzzled look.

Tom shrugged. "Strange hotels make for strange bedfellows."

Marianne calmly said, "Good evening, Mr. Moriarty. Excuse my *dishabille*."

"It delights the eye of an old man." Moriarty reseated himself after Marianne had slid into the booth.

Then Tom turned to her. "So, what happened?"

"I was abducted, to the basement."

"Lot of that going around. See anything?"

"A factory that makes automatons. They made one of me, an accurate duplicate. They did it with light, I think, though I don't know how it was done."

"Utterly intriguing." Moriarty's curiosity was piqued.

"I think I know what you may be talking about," Tom said. "Creeping technology, again. I'm beginning to suspect the Unseelie."

"It's so obvious an explanation that I have been reluctant to consider it," Moriarty said. "Too pat, too simple. I smell something even more ominous—though I have no doubt that the Unseelie may have seen to it that this sort of thing could happen."

"By seeing to it that some human magicians learn to practice the black arts as only the Unseelie can practice them?"

"Precisely," Moriarty said.

"What could be more ominous than that?"

"A melding of the black arts and the darkest forms of natural philosophy."

"Gotta admit, that would be formidable." Tom thumped a table with his fist. "We need Morrolan."

"An able enough magician," Moriarty said. "But is he adept in the darker disciplines?"

"You never know with Morrolan. He plays his hand close to the vest."

"A cable will take some time."

"We have other ways of communicating," Marianne said.

"I would be interested to know of these," Moriarty said.

"State secret," Tom added.

Moriarty smiled his smile, which was less a smile than a variation of *risus sardonicus*, the charming habit corpses have of baring their teeth. "Of course."

"As a matter of fact, he's standing by in case we need him," Marianne said.

"We shall need all the help we can get," Moriarty said.

"We?" Tom took a pull of his beer and said, "Excuse me, Professor Moriarty, but I didn't know we were allies."

"We must become allies, if we are not to be overwhelmed. If the world is not to be overwhelmed. By thunder, man, can't you see the gravity of the situation?"

"I can see that there's a robot factory downstairs that needs destroying. Other than that. . . ."

"Then you are a fool, Olam. You think this hotel is the center of operations? It is not."

"How do you know?"

"Because I have eyes and ears everywhere. I have my state secrets as well, Mr. Olam. From the intelligence gathered, I have concluded that the master control center is not here but elsewhere. And I harbor a suspicion as to the location."

"Where?"

"Mount Shasta."

"Mount Shasta? The extinct volcano?"

"The same. I believe Primus's lair is inside that mountain."

"Why do you suspect so?"

"Because of the unusual activity that has been reported in that area. Most of these wild stories we were talking about seem to have as their epicenter the isolated little hamlet of McCloud, which sits at the foot of the mountain. The only thing I haven't been able to figure out is why Primus did not pick a location nearer San Francisco. Mount Diablo, for instance."

"Shasta is a power source in two ways," Marianne put in. "Naturally and supernaturally."

Moriarty's eyes brightened. "I do believe you have the answer. Excellent, Mademoiselle."

"Then we'd better go there."

Moriarty leaned forward and asked delicately, "As allies?"

"As temporary allies."

"That is good. However, I should warn you—"

"You don't have to warn us," Tom said. "At any foot of the path, you reserve the right to turn on us."

"To pursue my own objectives," Moriarty said with a curl to his bloodless lips.

"Same thing." Tom upended his beer and drained it. "We'll see you in McCloud."

"By the way. A while back, you used an unusual word. 'Robot.' By that do you mean automaton?"

"Yes. Sorry, it's my time-tripping again. It's a term from the future."

"I was just thinking, there is a word in the Czech language.—"

"That's the word. Sorry, hard to explain."

Moriarty nodded in understanding. "You continue to amaze me, Olam. Not that your talents are negligible, but this mysterious dimension of yours makes you a man to be reckoned with. You are the most unusual man in the world. Aside from me, that is."

"Of course. Marianne, we've been rude. Do you want a drink?"

"Not here. I want to get out of this damned place."

"Right."

"May I offer you the use of my hotel room?" Moriarty said.

"Thanks, but we'd rather get our own," Marianne said.

"Very well. Until we meet again." Moriarty raised his glass and grinned amiably. It made Marianne shudder.

"I'm cold," she said. "Let's go."

They walked out of the bar and out of the Palace Hotel.

Ten

"I JUST WONDER what happened to John North," Tom said once he and Marianne were comfortably ensconced in a room at the Empire. Tom had run up to North's room and knocked, but no one answered.

Marianne, in a blue dressing gown, stood before the mirror of a vanity table. She wasn't looking at her reflection as much as looking *through* her reflection.

"You say you didn't run into him at the meeting. Are you sure he wasn't there?"

"No, can't be sure, because I was out of the room for most of it. He could have come in late, left early."

"Then that's probably what happened." Marianne bent closer to the mirror. "Morrolan? Are you there?"

"No," came a man's voice from the mirror.

Marianne laughed. "You are a silly person, Morrolan."

"So I've been told," Morrolan conceded.

"You're a little early," Marianne said.

"Then why are you standing there looking for me?"

"I spend a lot of time in front of mirrors. I am a woman, *n'est-ce pas*?"

"Knowing you as I now do, I will reserve comment."

Marianne hooded her eyes with a hand. "I can't see you clearly."

"Some disturbance in the ether, no doubt. What's up? Is Tom with you?"

"Right here," Tom said, standing to see the image of the sable-haired wizard wavering in the vanity mirror.

"Oh, there you are, Thomas. I say, that's a shabby sort of hotel room, if you don't mind my saying so. Isn't the place supposedly the best in town?"

"We're not at the Palace. Ran into some trouble. Place was overrun with mechanical dummies. Enchanted ones, we suspect."

"You don't say."

"We need your help, Morrolan," Marianne said.

Morrolan's face fell. "Oh, no. You don't mean . . ."

Tom nodded. "We need you here. Quick."

Morrolan pasted on a fatuous grin. "Well, you see, I have this previous engagement. Faerie woman, quite charming, really, invited me to a tenting holiday in the mountains, and of course being the outdoor type, naturally I . . ."

"Morrolan, we mean it," Tom said evenly. "There's some heavy magic brewing here, we think, and we need someone to scope it out."

"Damn. Well. Duty and all that. Let's see . . . San Francisco . . ."

"It's about eight and a half thousand miles from Munich, west-southwest."

Morrolan scowled. "My dear Thomas, distance and direction have nothing to do with traveling via the Faerie Veil. It's more a matter of interstitial energy and etheric resonance."

"Whatever you say. Can you pick a spot, or shall we pick one for you?"

"No reason I can't do a mirror walk and step right into your . . . well, your quarters there. I must prepare, though. A teleportation spell this big requires exacting specifications."

"I thought you said distance didn't matter."

"It doesn't. What matters is the smashing big magical vortex near you that brews even as we speak."

"Huh? You mean here, right here?"

"No. And not down the street either. Something quite big, and . . . I would say in the vicinity, but not too near."

"Mount Shasta, maybe?"

"Where?"

"Never mind, I'll explain when you arrive. How soon can you get here?"

"Give me an hour. No, two."

"Two enough?"

"Well, optimizing chances for success, the witching hour might be best."

"Which witching, your time or ours? It's midnight here."

"Greenwich mean."

"Why Greenwich mean?"

"Too complicated to explain."

Tom withdrew his pocket watch. "By my calculation, it's eight in the morning, Greenwich mean time."

Morrolan yawned. "Really? Haven't been to bed yet."

"Can you try it now?"

"Yes, if I have to," Morrolan said. "But I still need two hours to prepare."

"OK. We're going to get some sleep. Give a yell when you're ready to come through."

"Right. Cheerio."

When Morrolan's image faded from the mirror, Tom slumped to the bed. "I'm bushed."

Marianne threw herself almost comically on the covers. "I'm dead."

Tom rose. He tottered to the night table, thumbed off the lamp, collapsed on the bed, and fell fast asleep, by which time Marianne was already oblivious.

IN THE DARKENED room, faint motes of light drifted in the mirror, deep within its interior, swarming like moths on a summer night. They darted, flitted, merged, and divided again. The mirror no longer reflected the room. It was dark, save for the swarming lights. Over time, the lights brightened.

Then they coalesced into a blinding star whose points radiated outward in all directions, breaking the plane of the mirror's surface. Beams of light played about the room, taking the measure of the walls, floor, and ceiling, dancing across the figures on the bed.

Tom awoke with a start. He sat up, saw what was happening, and shook Marianne. She groaned.

"Wake up!" He jabbed a finger into her ribs, and her head popped up, eyes wide.

"Morrolan ever do this before?"

"No."

"Think we'd better exit the room for a while. I don't like the looks of this."

"Me neither."

"Crawl, don't let the beams touch you."

"I've been touched by these beams before," she said.

They crawled toward the door. Tom had the longer route, and Marianne waited.

Sounds were coming out of the mirror now, whooping, echoing sounds. Sounds never heard before. Frightening sounds.

"Go!" Tom said, leaping up and opening the door. Marianne slipped, and he hauled her up and threw her out into the hall. He succeeded in slamming the door shut a split second before the disturbance hit inside.

The sound was like nothing anything earthly could make. A howling combined with a mechanical clatter of metal. There came rending, smashing and tearing sounds, as though a team of demolition experts had materialized inside the room and gone instantly to work. Heavy things crashed against the door, nearly splitting it and tearing it off its hinges. It bulged, cracked, and warped, but held. There came the cracking of wood, the shattering of glass, the tearing of fabric, all at once in a concerto of destruction.

Then they heard a whirlwind sound, the rotation of a huge cyclone of devastation, while the other noise continued. Wind shrieked, thunder rumbled. Then, of a heart-stopping sudden, the din ceased utterly.

Tom and Marianne had retreated down the hall.

Doors began opening along the length of the corridor. Sleepy heads showed, mouths complaining.

"What the devil's the ruckus?"

"Something outside," Tom announced. "Passing thunderstorm."

"But it sounded like it came from next door. Your room."

"Nothing's going on in our room," Tom said, laughing.

"Damned nuisance, I say! People are trying to sleep!"

"Sorry. Nothing to be alarmed about. Go back to bed."

Lame, Tom thought.

He gingerly placed a hand on the doorknob and twisted. He pushed, and the door came away from its hinges and crashed into the room.

He looked in. The room was a complete shambles. Not only was just about everything else in pieces, but most of the plaster had crumbled from the walls, revealing the laths. The room was gutted. Even the floorboards had been torn up. The only thing intact was the vanity and its mirror, in perfect condition.

And standing in the middle of it all was Morrolan in his wizard's robes, carrying bag in hand.

Setting down the bag, he shrugged apologetically. "Have I come at a bad time?"

Eleven

THE NEXT MORNING, Tom, Marianne, and Morrolan boarded a train on the Bear Flag Rail Road for Sacramento, booking a private coach. The car looked brand new, the rail was in fine shape, and the train maintained a steady twenty-five miles an hour.

The trip went fine until Tom caught sight of Sam Clemens in the dining car.

"I don't like it," he said, finishing the last of his wine. "He's got something to do with all this."

"Well, he can't do anything on the train," Morrolan said. "Can he?"

"What's he doing here? I saw him at the hotel, now he's here. He must be following us."

"Methinks thou'rt becoming too suspicious, Tom," Morrolan said with a smile.

"I'm not paranoid."

Morrolan frowned. "Whatever does that mean?"

"Never mind. Let's get back to the coach, and let's keep our hands on our guns."

"I don't have one."

"Well, work up a spell or something."

"I trust guns more than spells," Marianne said. "Let's go."

"I knew there was something I liked about you," Tom said.

They made their way back through the cars, keeping an eye out for suspicious characters, especially for anyone familiar who might have been at the hotel.

As Tom approached the door to their compartment, two men were coming the other way. Tom studied their faces. The one in the lead had a strange look, and in the dim light the face was masklike. Something was not natural about it.

Tom let the man have it straight in the snoot, then collared the other one and cocked his fist back.

The man held up his hands and pleaded, "Please, sir, we didn't do anything!"

He was visibly frightened. Uncertain, Tom let him go.

The one Tom had punched picked himself up.

Tom rubbed two fingers against the man's face, and saw that something had come off. A beige smudge. Makeup. The man's nose was bleeding. "I'm sorry," Tom said.

"Smallpox," the man said. "Is there a crime in wearing stage makeup to cover a pockmarked face? You, sir, are a cad and a ruffian. My seconds will call on you in the morning."

"Uh . . . OK. Look, I'm very sorry. Here, take my handkerchief."

"The very least you can do, sir," the man said. He snagged the handkerchief and dabbed his nose flamboyantly.

"Uh . . . all I can say is that I thought you were a couple of thugs that we—"

"He calls us thugs! We are *actors*, sir. Artists!"

"Outrageous!" said the other one. "We shall complain to the conductor! To the railroad!"

"You are an insensate bully, sir!"

"Philistine!"

Tom watched them march indignantly down the corridor. Morrolan and Marianne were looking at him balefully.

He shrugged. "OK, maybe I'm hallucinating. I'm paranoid."

"I'm going to have to look that word up," Morrolan murmured to Marianne as they entered the compartment. She shrugged.

"Don't worry, Tom," she said inside. "What I saw in that hotel cellar wasn't a hallucination."

"We won't be boarding the train north," Tom said.

"Why not?" Morrolan said.

"We're going to buy horses, camping gear, and ride up to McCloud."

"Egads. What on earth for?"

"We're too vulnerable on a train. Too easy to get us separated. Maybe I've seen too many Alfred Hitchcock movies."

Tom's companions just looked at each other.

"Anyway, that's what we'll do."

"Would you mind if I took the train alone?" Morrolan asked. "I don't much care for horseback riding. Besides, I don't have a proper riding outfit."

"You can get it in Sacramento," Tom said.

"But surely it's the last outpost of civilization. Anyway, don't they have strange ways of riding out here in the West? Neck reining. Barbaric. Why, I wouldn't know the first thing about riding a cowboy horse."

"You'll learn. You'll be riding like a cowpuncher in no time."

"I'm a slow learner. Besides, I've never punched a cow."

I CAN'T SAY what it was, exactly," Morrolan said as his horse plodded along the trail through the ponderosa pines. He was dressed in a very snappy riding outfit: doeskin riding breeches, boots, wool coat, and felt hat, all English, all purchased at a chic tack shop on Sacramento's version of Rodeo Drive. "Except to repeat that it got through the mirror before me, and tried to block my way. I suppose that doesn't help."

"Not a whole hell of a lot," Tom said. "It must have been hellish, though." His horse was a bit more spirited and was threatening to break into a canter. He drew back on the reins.

"What, the thing itself or dealing with it?"

"Both."

"Of course it was hellish. And as I've said several times now, I was quite astonished by it. I'd never seen its like before in the interstices between the universes."

"It was a killing machine," Marianne said. "Sent to kill us." She had bought suitable riding clothes, too, but they were more conventional for the time and locale: dungarees, Western boots, blue cotton shirt, brown leather vest, and a wide-brim black hat. At her waist, a simple leather holster held a Colt Navy side arm.

"Yes, but it had a uniquely magical dimension to it," Morrolan said. "In and of itself."

"I wouldn't be surprised."

"Both mechanical and magical," Tom mused. "Interesting."

"A machine with an extra dimension. Or perhaps. . . ."

Tom let Morrolan ruminate for an interval. "What?"

"Perhaps a magical construct. A nonmaterial machine."

"You mean a conjuration?"

"No. Nothing so mundane. What I'm talking about is a machine built of nonmaterial parts. Of course, when it manifests itself, it does so in terms of gears and levers and such. Do you grasp the concept?"

"Not quite."

"I'll work on it. Anyway, I haven't the foggiest what to do with it, how to fight it. You can't fight what you don't completely understand. By the way. . . ."

Marianne's roan mare was acting up, whickering and getting skittish. Tom wondered if simply talking about such things spooked the horses. Or perhaps somebody or something was nearby, watching.

"You were saying, Morrolan?"

"How far did you say it is to this little town. What's it called? MacLeod?"

"You're giving it a Scots pronunciation. McCloud."

"Yes. How far?"

"About two hundred miles."

"Good *God*." Morrolan's tongue hung out as he rolled his eyes. "Well, we shall simply have to do something about that."

"Such as? You said the vortex would prevent you from zipping us there."

"Yes, but there are other ways. Let me think a moment."

"Do so," Tom said. "I'm not particularly savoring the prospect of a two-hundred-mile trip on horse-back."

"Neither is my derriere," Marianne said.

Morrolan grinned. "Have I ever told you, Marianne, that I studied the art of massage from a Hindu masseuse, when I was in India?"

Marianne smiled slyly. "Have I ever told you that I studied the art of silent killing from a Japanese master assassin?"

"Uh, no. You must tell me all about it . . . sometime."

Tom was ruminating. "I just wonder if we could have persuaded anyone to leave that convention."

"With stories about automatons in the cellar?" Marianne scoffed. "Not a chance."

Tom sighed. "I guess you're right. Better to try to knock out the source of the conspiracy." Tom's black gelding took a few more steps before he added, "Not that we have a clue as to how to go about doing it."

"Oh, we'll think of something," Morrolan said. "But first we'd better think about the person or persons following us."

Tom gave a quick look back. "Are you sure? More than one, do you think?"

"I'm sure. Can't isolate the number, but it's not a gang."

"Then let's get off the trail and wait for them."

This the three riders did, stationing themselves behind some sapling firs at the base of a hillock off the trail to the right.

Presently, John North, astride a piebald gelding, came riding up the trail.

Tom galloped out to meet him, holstering his pistol.

"Tom! Looks like I let myself get ambushed."

"Where've you been, John? I was looking for you at that meeting."

"Came late. It was quite a meeting, wasn't it? Who's this?"

"John North, this is Morrolan, an associate of ours."

"My pleasure. Magician, aren't you? Think I've heard of you." North touched his hat. "This must be the countess. *Enchanté*, mademoiselle."

"A pleasure, Mr. North."

"Well, shall we all ride together? Might be a bad idea, actually."

"No, I think under the circumstances, it'd be best to team up," Tom said. "The opposition might be formidable. Numbers might help."

"You're right. OK, I'd be delighted. Let me take the point for now." North took out a pocket watch. "We should think about making camp in about two hours."

"Are there. . . ." Morrolan began.

"Yes?" North said, reining his horse back.

"Are there many snakes about these parts?"

"Several varieties."

"Venomous sorts, I take it."

"One or two kinds. Why?"

"Just curious."

Marianne's lips turned up in a smile. "Morrolan, I didn't know you were afraid of anything."

"Afraid? No, old girl, I was thinking of what I need for a certain spell I want to work on."

"Oh, I see."

"Snakes are talismans to the Red Indians. Thought I'd best work in that idiom."

"Good idea," Tom said. "Let's get going."

NO TRADITIONAL CAMPFIRE scene. They dined on beef jerky and hardtack, then bedded down amongst rocks up the side of a hill, the horses tethered to one side, huddled in some bushes.

Morrolan took to the woods alone.

"What's he doing out there?" Tom wondered.

Marianne was curled up on her bed of pine needles.

"Chasing newts and one-eyed toads and such things. For his magic."

"Alone. Guy has nerves of steel. There are dangerous animals around here. Aren't there, John?"

"Sure are. Black bears. Grizzlies. Mountain lions."

"Dangerous enough."

"I don't know about bears, but I've never seen the cat that didn't purr under Morrolan's hand," Marianne said. "He can charm any beast."

"I'm not worried about beasts so much," Tom said. "But Moriarty's out there somewhere. He's probably following us."

"Probably hatching another tall tale," North said. "The one he told you was a lulu."

"Yeah, well, it was likely an equal mixture of truth and lies. But there has to be. . . . Listen, instead of kicking it around once more, let's get some sleep."

"Good idea," North said. "Good night."

"Good night."

Tom rolled over. In other times, in other circumstances, he would have relished a camping trip. The smell of pine was sweet and strong, the air scrubbed as fresh as it comes, quiet blanketing all. It was early in the summer, and only a few crickets strummed. The forest was still, not a branch stirring.

It would be nice to go camping with Marianne, he thought. Just the two of them. Nothing went with the great outdoors like a great woman. And Marianne was certainly that. Tom's thoughts drifted back over the last few years of their association, the most eventful years in his life, all the way back to the day he toured Neuschwanstein castle in Bavaria. While walking innocently around the Meistersinger's Hall—gaping in wonder at the rococo splendor and asking himself what kind of king would build for himself a castle out of fairy tale by way of Walt Disney World—he was suddenly spellnapped into a strange new Bavaria in an even stranger Europe, one that seemed to be one part *Lord of the Rings* and two parts Jules Verne's science fiction, with a little bit of *Prisoner of Zenda* thrown in. New Europa was a place that the Victorian Age should have been and more, a reality where high magic lived side by side with weird inventions out of an Industrial Revolution on LSD. It was an age of high adventure, as well. Bavaria—Bayern—was ruled by an evil regent, whom Tom helped to depose, replacing him with King Ludwig II, the king who built Neuschwanstein in Tom's universe, and who immediately proceeded to build—with faerie magic—Castle Falkenstein, his wildest dream to date.

Tom's sojourn in New Europa had been nonstop adventure all the way. Exciting. Too exciting, sometimes.

Like now, with someone or something tramping out of the woods. A twig snapped. Tom's Colt revolver was out quick, cocked and ready.

He saw Morrolan's shape advancing in the moonlight.

Morrolan dropped something in front of Tom. "Watch these for me," he said. "I've got to go out again."

"What are they?"

"Three dried rats."

"Dried rats. Uh, where were they, you know . . . dried?"

"In a cave, nearby. Now I need to go back in there and wait for the bats to come back. Need a bat."

"Don't bats stay out at night?"

"They'll return before dawn if they've munched enough bugs."

"Rats, bats. What else do you need?"

"Well, actually, not just any bat. A pipistrelle would be ideal. And voles do better than plain field rats. But these will do. Don't let anything eat them."

"No snacking, right."

"Sleep well."

Morrolan melded with the darkness again.

"Guy has style," Tom said, snuggling back into his bedroll.

Falkenstein. What a world....

He had just about dozed off when something gently jolted him back. He lifted his head, but heard only quiet. Then he shrugged and settled back in.

He heard it again. Rather, he felt it, through the ground.

A tremor?

Yes, a tremor, the beats coming fairly regular now. One . . . two . . . three . . . four . . . like footsteps. Big footsteps.

Very big footsteps.

The ground began to tremble. Something was walking out there in the trees. Something huge, weighing tons.

Coming up the trail.

Marianne and North were already on their feet.

"What's your guess?" Tom asked.

"Got me," North said. "Whatever it is, let's not be here when it arrives."

Morrolan came running out of the woods. "Shall we be toddling off now? I've saddled the horses."

"What's out there?"

Morrolan mounted up. "Don't worry. Just ride and hope the spell works."

"What spell?"

"On the horses."

"But you just said you needed—"

"That was an hour ago. Ride!"

They rode.

What chased them through the forest was at first hard to grasp. Something on a huge scale, tramping with thunderous steps. Marianne chanced a look back and saw an immense, manlike shape, as tall as the ponderosas. A giant, made of something that gleamed in the moonlight. Metal.

A giant automaton.

As fast as the four rode, as fast as the horses could gallop, the monstrosity behind them continued to close the gap. Its stride, taking up huge lengths of trail with each step, could have been measured in furlongs. Trees were to it like weeds—merely things to be trampled, pushed aside, or uprooted, no matter how thick the forest and undergrowth. No matter where the foursome led it—up and down hills, off the trail and through bramble—in an effort to go where it could not, it made no difference. The metal monster's speed did not slacken in the least.

Tom looked back. As the mechanical Gargantua pounded along, wisps of steam escaped from its head.

A steam-powered automaton. Had the thing walked all the way from San Francisco? Or was Primus's base somewhere near?

Or was Lord Tomino, who had conquered northern Japan with just this sort of gadget, really Primus?

These questions raced through Tom's mind as he rode, but he didn't expect ever to have an answer, for in just a few moments he would be pressed like meat beneath the pedal extremities of an improbable mechanical giant, a thing incongruous in this sylvan setting.

No time to wonder how it had materialized—in all likelihood it had done just that—or to guess who had done the trick. There was only time to dig in heels and ride. Tom was doubtful, though, that the horses had any more to give.

Then, as if wanting to prove him wrong, his horse seemed to put on an additional burst of speed. Then more.

Suddenly and quite unbidden, his mount jumped into the air and began to fly. The trail fell away, then the tops of trees went by, and Tom, barely able to believe it was happening, was airborne.

The horse did not sprout wings, and it did not so much fly as leap in impossible, gigantic bounds, vaulting from the crest of one hill to the next.

Out of the corner of his eye, Tom saw that the other horses were similarly magicked. Why the riders were not thrown off immediately was a mystery, but Tom hadn't the presence of mind to ponder it.

The four of them rode like demons out of hell, like Valkyrie, like ancient Greeks on horse-gods, thundering through long valleys in minutes, leaping arroyos thirty yards wide. Miles melted away.

The wind was cold and bracing, and the stars wheeled above. (They really did look to be moving, and Tom wondered if some kind of time-contraction effect was operative.) After the initial shock and amazement, Tom settled down and enjoyed the ride. He seemed to be having no trouble staying on the horse, no matter what the speed, no matter how violent the sudden accelerations. Magic, he supposed. It was all magic. Funny, in this world where magic and science were almost equal, he always felt a slight sense of guilt when he benefited from the former. It was like cheating, in a sense, though he couldn't put his finger on a good reason for his feeling this way.

Time passed. He cast another look backward. The horses were raising huge clouds of dust that billowed up to obscure the stars. If anybody was massing behind the robot to attack, they'd have trouble finding their objective.

No sign of the big clanking thing.

Colors were strange. The night was transfigured: the sky brooded in purple, the stars had a bluish cast, and shadows harbored red pulsings and filaments of half-perceived light. Things got more bizarre as time passed and miles fell away. Streaks of odd colors went whistling by, and a purple haze gathered in the underbrush. Soon, bursts of light blossomed in the sky, and great, winged birds of light flapped by. Generally, magically speaking, the spell was getting out of hand, or so Tom thought.

Or fizzling. Maybe just wearing out.

"Spell's about run its course," Morrolan announced as the mounts slowed to a loping canter. "We'd best rest the horses. If they survive."

Tom halted his mount and got off. Rivers of foam ran from its back down the flanks, and its breath sounded like the chugging of a steam engine. White smoke shot out its nostrils.

"These horses are about done in," Tom said. He unstrapped his bedroll and covered the beast with the blanket.

"There's the chance they'll collapse and die," Morrolan worried, despite his distaste for the group's mode of transport. "More magic. I'll take care of it."

"If we don't take care of these poor beasts, they'll catch their death," Marianne said.

"I said I'll take care of it," Morrolan repeated, a little irritably.

"That was the most amazing thing I've ever experienced," North enthused. "Fantastic!"

Marianne's horse sank to its knees.

"Oh, dear," she said. "Poor beast."

Morrolan rose after examining the creature. "It will be fine. Don't worry."

Tom was looking rearward. "Must have left that thing miles behind."

"A good hundred," Morrolan ventured.

"Still, a hundred miles to that thing. . . ."

"I'd hazard a guess it gave up," Morrolan said.

"That means we can get some rest ourselves," Tom said, dragging up a log. "Here's a nice pillow."

"Charming. Well, this is America. The Great Out-doors, and all that sort of rubbish."

"Every day is Earth Day in California."

"Eh? Olam, you say the strangest things."

"By the way, nice spell."

"Why, thank you. I suppose you're not so very strange, after all."

Twelve

WHATEVER EXTRA MAGIC Morrolan had whipped up to save the horses, it seemed to work. The mounts had recovered by morning, generally none the worse for extreme wear. However, they could not bring themselves to do more than mope along the trail for most of the day. The riders walked along beside them.

"No more enchanting these poor brutes," Morrolan said. "At least not for a while."

"Have another trick up your sleeve?" Tom asked.

"A few."

"Want us to hunt rats for you? Find snakes, lizards?"

"If I need anything, I'll let you know."

"How come magic stuff is always so gross and disgusting?"

"*Chacun à son goût*, eh, Marianne?"

"*Vraiment*," Marianne agreed.

"There is something you could do for me," Morrolan said.

"Name it."

"I need to know exactly where this little village is."

"I have a map right here in my saddlebag," North said.

"May I examine it, please?"

"Certainly."

"There you go with position and distance again," Tom chided.

"Should we go into McCloud at all?" Marianne wondered.

"She's right," Tom said to North. "Ten to one it's chock full of automatons."

"Good bet," North said. "But . . . have any idea how we get up the mountain without mountain-climbing gear?"

"No," Tom said. "You have a point. We need rope and suchlike. Have you ever done any mountain climbing?"

"Not a lot," North said. "We're really improvising, aren't we?"

"A bit. Figure the entrance to the hideout is at the summit?"

"Summit's at fourteen thousand feet. It'll be impossible to get that high. But there could be caves along the slope."

"In a volcanic cone?"

"Fumaroles," North said. "Vents. Lava tubes."

"Right, but they could still be venting sulfurous fumes."

"Just a little. The volcano's been extinct for more than a hundred years."

"Not long, geologically speaking. Sounds iffy. What do you think, Marianne?"

"There are glaciers on the mountain. We could freeze if we don't have proper attire."

"Not at this time of year," Tom said. "In winter, we'd freeze to death, but in June we'd just chatter, get pneumonia, and then die."

Marianne laughed. Morrolan looked up from the map. "We're going to what?"

"In any event, we'll have to work the town to get any information," Tom added.

"I wonder what information we can get from automatons," Marianne said.

"We shall see," Tom said.

North was peering up ahead. "I'm seeing a glint of metal up on that ridge."

Tom looked up and saw a flash. Almost instantaneously, a terrific explosion tore up the forest behind them. The horses neighed and reared.

Tom scanned the ridge. Sure enough, several cannon barrels protruded from the trees.

Then the barrels began to move down the slope. They belonged to huge, lumbering land fortresses, crashing through the trees. Tanks, as Tom would have called them in his home world. Steam-driven, nineteenth-century tanks.

The four riders beat a hasty retreat over the hill they had just crested. Morrolan rode holding the unfolded map behind him, fluttering in the wind. Halfway up the slope, he lost it, and it went billowing back toward the advancing tank column.

"Blast! Sorry about that," Morrolan said when the four had regrouped.

"Can we make it around this valley?" Tom asked.

North scanned the encompassing mountains. "It's going to be hard, Tom."

"And we have nothing to go up against land fortresses."

"All too true," North conceded.

"So we'll have to detour around them."

"It'll take days."

"Got no choice," Tom said. Then he saw his wizard friend riding away. "Morrolan, where are you going?"

"Follow," Morrolan said.

Tom, North, and Marianne looked at each other. They shrugged. They followed.

"He looks like he knows what he's doing," Tom said. "I like that in a man."

Morrolan led them back down into the hollow they had just ridden out of, the trail twisting through giant firs.

"Whoever's orchestrating the opposition," Tom said, "doesn't know much about tank tactics. This terrain is not ideal for land fortress warfare."

"Those things look like they could bull their way through any forest."

"Let's hope these particular machines are more conventional than they are magical."

They came upon the mouth of a cave. Morrolan led the way in. It was just big enough for the four riders to enter without ducking their heads. The chamber inside widened greatly and looked like it had been excavated.

Marianne sniffed. "I smell dragons."

"Yes," Morrolan said. "I spotted it as we came up the mountain."

Light from the cave's mouth dimmed quickly, and soon the horses refused to go any farther. The riders dismounted.

"Now what?" Tom asked.

"I don't know," Morrolan said. "I don't know any North American dragons personally. I'll have to play this one by ear. Let's keep walking. The horses will be fine."

They walked a good distance across the cavern. Suddenly, a gout of flame erupted from the darkness ahead.

"Come no farther!" a booming voice warned.

"Hello!" Morrolan called cheerily. "Just dropped in for a visit. Don't want to trouble you."

Another plume of flame illuminated the huge chamber. "Who dares to enter the lair of Orifex, Lord of the Sierra?"

"Morrolan here. Friend of His Majesty Verithrax Draconis."

"So say you. What proof have you of this purported friendship with the king of dragons?"

"I wear a gold medallion with his signet inscribed. A gift from the king, betokening our bond of trust."

A smaller tongue of flame briefly blossomed, and then a steadier flame took its place. It came from a torch held by an immense, winged figure. The creature did not have arms or hands as such: dewclaws, sprouting a third of the way along the creature's capacious wings, grasped the torch. The dragon walked upright on big, taloned feet. It advanced out of the darkness, drawing close to Morrolan, who held the medallion up by its gold chain. The dragon's saurian face, horrifically demonic, showed its descent from the great reptiles of the Jurassic. Yet, there was something else in the face, too—a great, benign intelligence, among other surprising qualities.

The dragon peered at Morrolan's medal. Then it said, "You should have said something first thing. I was going to toast you on general principles. Ever since humans discovered the gold in these parts, we've had any number of intruders. Come back, please. I am Lord Orifex. Any friend of Verithrax is a friend of mine."

"Thank you," said Morrolan. "Actually, we would ask for asylum. Hostile forces without seek to destroy us."

"I did hear something. There's big magic brewing at a sacred mountain to the north of here."

"That is our destination."

"Truly? Then you take a great risk. The sorcery that I sense there is like nothing I've ever experienced. I have not divined its nature, or its source. Have you?"

"We're not altogether sure," Morrolan said.

"You are welcome to stay here as long as you like. I don't mind human guests. However, king's friend or not, I must warn you that if I find any of my treasure missing, the slightest gewgaw or bauble—this goes for any of you—you'll be rendered down to crisps of fat. Understood?"

"Clear enough," Morrolan said cheerily. "Come along, friends."

As they walked farther into the cave, it became apparent that they had entered a vast system of caverns, complete with stalagmites and stalactites, limestone pillars, side passages, galleries, and various other rooms. It was a warren. It was, in fact, a dragon's lair.

Gold and silver glinted in the gloom. The place overflowed with treasure: jewels and precious metals of all sorts, fabricated into an endless assortment of artifacts. There were other objets d'art, as well: statuary, sculpture, even some paintings.

"Lots of nice stuff," Tom said.

"Dragons have taste," Marianne said.

They did not stop to examine any of it. It would hardly have been politic. Besides, Orifex strode purposefully on into the warren, leading the way, and it was hard enough just keeping up with him.

Finally, the main passage debouched into a huge cathedral chamber bathed in torchlight. Fine rugs graced the smooth rock floor. Orifex welcomed his guests, ushering them to big, comfortable high-backed chairs carved with ancient draconic runes. Orifex took his seat in the biggest chair.

There was more clutter all around: chests of gold and platinum, ancient shields and masks, spears and other weapons, hides and animals heads. A fire crackled in a hearth to one side.

"May I offer you food and drink?" Orifex asked.

"Certainly," Morrolan said.

"Dragons eat their cousins," Orifex said. "Birds. Humans eat them, too, which is why I have no qualms about offering you same."

Another dragon, somewhat smaller than Orifex, entered the room.

"Bring food and drink," Orifex commanded, and the servant bowed and left, exiting via one of many side passages.

"How may I help you, Morrolan, friend of Verithrax?"

"We're trying to reach the human village of McCloud."

"Ah. And obstacles of a magical nature, I take it, block your way. I'm afraid there is not much I can do. I am a poor magician. I collect art, and do little else."

"Do these caves of yours continue in a northerly direction?" Tom asked.

"They do."

"Is there an exit perhaps at the farthest end?"

"There are several, in fact. You may walk through at your leisure, if this will enable you to skirt danger. However, I'm not sure your animals would fit through some of the narrower passages."

"I could spell the animals to meet us," Morrolan said, "but if anything went wrong, we'd be stranded."

"But thank you for the offer, Orifex," Tom said.

"It is nothing," Orifex said. "How else may I serve you?"

"May we stay the night?" Morrolan asked.

"My cave is your cave," Orifex said. "However, this does not seem entirely helpful."

"True," Tom said. "We'll get a breather, but we'll face the same problem in the morning."

Morrolan sighed and leaned forward. "Do you have any suggestions, Orifex?"

"Let me ponder the problem," Orifex said as the servant arrived bearing a tray. "First, let us drink. I think you will find this wine to your liking. It is sweet, made of fermented alpine clover honey. It has a delicate, yet exquisite taste."

The servant poured the drinks and left. Tom tasted his wine. It was thick, syrupy, and could hardly be called delicate. He set his glass down on one of many side tables, each garishly carved and inlaid. Dragons had taste, all right, but different tastes. The wine's bouquet reminded him of freshly mowed hay fields. Not unpleasant, but not the kind of thing you'd want with . . . what was this? Birds? Trays of birds.

Whole birds, roasted, on gold plates. All sizes of avian: small, medium, large. All were room temperature.

"Pardon these leftovers," Orifex said. "All we have on hand."

"Uh, what are these?" Marianne asked.

Orifex looked the assortment over. "Oh, night-hawk, osprey, loon, thrasher, owl, turkey vulture . . . let's see, lots here . . . that's a bobwhite, I think . . . tasty, tasty . . . and this is an eagle."

"Eagle?"

"Delicious, but of course the real savor comes from eating them on the wing, you know. You flame them from below, all the feathers burn right up, and the bird drops right into your mouth. Crunch, crunch, all in one motion. Now, that's eating. This way is more civilized, but rather joyless. Do try some."

"Uh. . . ." Marianne picked up a small bird that she hoped was a duck, tore off a leg. She took a bite, then nodded, a little surprised. "Wonderful. What is it?"

"Coot."

"Coot?"

"Coot."

Marianne swallowed hard. "Very . . . very good."

"I'm glad you like it. Tell me, Morrolan, what news have you of my European cousins?"

Morrolan launched into a long news report while Tom, North, and Marianne continued to pick at cold, flame-broiled birds. Some were palatable, others gamy, and a few downright rank, having a taste that put one in mind of kerosene.

This was not human food, Marianne thought. But how could one expect otherwise? Dragons had humanlike qualities, but they had enjoyed a separate evolutionary development going back millions of years.

"I have it!" Orifex said, interrupting Morrolan's report. "We'll fly you to McCloud."

"Fly?" Tom said. "You mean by dragon?"

"Yes. I don't mean myself, of course. There is a great-winged dragon of my acquaintance who owes me a favor. Uh . . . you are aware that dragons come in racial varieties?"

"Yes," Tom said. "But I was under the impression that great-winged dragons resented being used as transportation."

"True, ordinarily. A proud people, greats are. 'I am no conveyance' is the usual demurral you hear. But Garsprinilla is rather heavily in my debt, the details of which I am not at liberty to divulge. Clan matters . . . family. She will be here in the morning to carry you—not without some complaining, I must warn you—to the human settlement of McCloud. And now. . . ."

Orifex rose and stretched his wings, then flapped them a few times. The resulting wind nearly swept the remains of the supper off the tables.

"Pardon me. I really must retire. I do hope you find your quarters comfortable. Good night."

The guests rose and watched their host exit the great chamber.

"Nice guy," Tom said.

"Rather," Morrolan said. "Are you ready for a dragon ride?"

"It might be fun," Marianne said. "Unless you're afraid of heights."

"Who, me?" Morrolan said skeptically. "You're talking to a man who's flown on straw brooms."

"What about the horses?" North asked.

"I can lay a spell on them," Morrolan said. "There's a one in five chance they'll trot into McCloud a few days after we get there."

"We can always get fresh mounts, as long as we have the money," Tom said.

"If McCloud still exists," North said. "If it's not a ghost town."

Thirteen

I N THE MORNING they breakfasted on more dreadful cold bird and a curious hot herb beverage; then, on instruction, they saddled their horses and prepared to climb to the top of the mountain that harbored Orifex's lair. Orifex himself made an appearance shortly before their departure.

"I wouldn't advise falling off Garsprinilla's back," the dragon lord said. "She won't dive to save you. I will have my servants fetch dragon saddles up the hill to you, and they will see to it that Garsprinilla is saddled properly. Strap yourselves in securely. Your safety is your responsibility."

"We are in your debt, Orifex," Morrolan said.

"Think nothing of it. My apologies for not seeing you off personally, but I must leave forthwith on a business trip south. I doubt your adversaries will try anything with Garsprinilla. Even supernatural forces do not lightly provoke a great, as they are the most powerful magicians among us."

"Thanks for the hospitality," Tom said as he left the cave.

"Enjoy the trip," Orifex said, raising one wing.

The journey to the mountaintop was a pleasant horse ride. Nothing impeded their way. No attack came out of the trees, no mechanical curiosities made a bid to intercept. The morning air was crisp and, as always in these parts, tinged with the odor of pine.

Dragon servants awaited them at the rocky summit, four in all, each bearing an immense saddle.

Tom had seen great-winged dragons before, but never close-up. He wondered just how big greats got.

He and his companions soon found out. A winged figure appeared in the sky, circling, getting progressively lower. Its outline grew and grew, and all were amazed by the wingspan. Tom estimated the creature to be fully fifty feet from wing tip to wing tip. The scaled body, green with flecks of gilt here and there, was about thirty feet long.

Aerodynamically impossible, Tom thought. Can't fly. Ah, but that's why greats were spectacularly adept magicians. They flew by magic, not Bernoulli's principle. (An oversimplification, for dragon wings supplied *some* lift, but not enough to keep the dragon airborne without supernatural help.)

The creature bore down, flapping her mighty wings, and alighted on a rounded outcropping. As the servants began to strap on the saddles, Garsprinilla's head came around to examine her prospective passengers, her gimlet gaze raking them. The face was capable of much expression, in a saurian way. A sardonic sort of sneer curled the toothy mouth.

"So, you're the deadheads who want a free ride?"

"That's us," said Morrolan. "Unless we're putting you out greatly."

"Oh, no trouble at all. I have nothing better to do than to haul two-legged monkeys off to some jerkwater town for no earthly reason I can see. What's wrong? Are you lazy, or physically handicapped in some way? Or just craven?"

"We have encountered some opposition on our journey," Morrolan explained. "We believe we are in considerable danger."

"Oh, so you are cowards."

"Please," Tom said. "Intestinally challenged. "

"Fine circumlocution. I'll have to remember that. Well, climb aboard. And if you empty your intestines all over my back, or pull any other cute tricks, I'll unload the lot of you on a handy cloud."

"No crap, and that's a promise," Tom assured the creature.

"Very well. Now, let's get going, if you don't mind so awfully much."

The saddles, lined up in pairs along a row of sharp fins down the beast's back, were fairly complicated affairs, but the upshot was that the rider had to ride sidesaddle, one leg crooked around a post. A safety belt went around the rider's waist. For added security, one could grasp leather handholds, or hold on to the fins, but these latter were rather sharp, and tended to move with the beast's exertions.

In any event, it was clear that riding a dragon was not for the faint of heart.

Tom and Marianne took the rear pair of seats and wrapped their arms about each other. North and Morrolan made do with the handholds.

Without bothering to ask if her fares were ready, the creature abruptly bolted, jumped off the shear cliff on the northern side of the mountain, and plummeted alarmingly before its wings caught the air. Like some great unlikely bird, the beast bore upward in a long, slow spiral, its great, leathery wings flapping, their sound like the luffing of a schooner's sails.

As the dragon climbed, the view became magnificent. A line of distant, snow-capped peaks led north: the Cascade Range, a row of volcanic cones stretching all the way up into Canada. Lassen Peak, the first, was plainly visible, but Tom wasn't sure if he could pick out Shasta yet. To the east lay the Sierras, their snows all melted this time of year. It had been a warm spring.

The temperature dropped precipitously as the dragon gained a high altitude and headed north, borne aloft by rising thermals. There was no sound but the wind. The almost-silence was eerie.

"I thought we were going to need oxygen," Tom said to Marianne.

"I'm cold," she said.

"So am I."

They hugged each other tighter.

The dragon had flown about twenty miles north when Morrolan pointed to the left and said, "What the blazes is that?"

Tom and Marianne looked. A strange aircraft, looking like a cross between a helicopter and an aeroplane, was approaching quickly. Neither fish nor fowl, it had huge, fixed wings, several sets of them in fact, and two sets of whirling blades overhead.

"Auto-gyro, I think," Tom said.

"What?"

"Heavier-than-air flying machine," Tom said.

The craft swooped up behind the dragon. A burst of Gatling-gun fire came from it. The weapon had an unusually rapid rate of fire, sounding like the buzzing of an angry bumblebee.

A hail of bullets hissed over the passengers' heads, and Garsprinilla banked crazily to the left and went into a dive. The auto-gyro followed, and Tom was chagrined to see how maneuverable the strange craft was. With that Gatling, you could hardly miss.

But Garsprinilla carried a full bag of tricks. For the next several minutes she dog-fought with the auto-gyro, banking, turning, even looping once, and doing all with the agility of a modern high-tech fighter. The passengers grimly held on, but Morrolan's safety strap came loose and he slid from the saddle, saving himself with the handholds only. North reached over and hauled him back.

Garsprinilla went through a series of loops and dives. Tom lost all orientation. When his head stopped swimming, he saw that the dragon had maneuvered herself behind and above her adversary. The auto-gyro banked sharply back and forth, but Garsprinilla stayed with it.

Suddenly, with a hissing roar, a tremendous gout of flame shot out of her mouth and engulfed the strange aeroship. The flames, like liquid fire, dripped off viscously. The dragon equivalent of napalm, Tom thought.

"How's that for projectile vomiting?" Tom said in Marianne's ear. She didn't smile.

The aeroship began to burn and plummet, veering off at a sharp angle. It looked completely out of control. Tom followed its descent but eventually lost it in some low-flying clouds. He continued to keep an eye out for an explosion or fire or smoke, but none appeared. Perhaps, he thought, the pilot had pulled out of the death dive.

Not a good idea, attacking a dragon in flight.

They flew on. Lassen Peak, barren and snow-capped, fell away below. Other volcanic features dotted the landscape: cones, water-filled craters, dark lava flows, lighter slides of ash and rock, and inundations of pumice. Between small patches of trees, the land looked as barren and primordial as that of some Arctic realm: Iceland or parts of the Bering archipelago. This was a region of unstable geology, part of the ring of fire that ran along the grinding juncture of the Pacific and North American tectonic plates. From that titanic friction was born the fires of volcanism that ringed the Pacific Ocean. This region was only a small part of it. Northward, in what in Tom's universe would become the state of Washington, Mount St. Helens sat in brooding inactivity. He wondered if the mountain would erupt in this universe. Or would it be Mount Hood, or Mount Rainier? Geological events are mostly a matter of chance. Perhaps Shasta itself was next to go. As North had noted, the last eruption of Shasta had been in the eighteenth century, a little less than a hundred years ago. Beyond that, Tom didn't know much about the mountain's volcanic history, his knowledge of the Cascade volcanoes being sketchy, to say the least.

He was betting, and hoping, that Shasta was a dormant volcano, if not an extinct one.

There it was ahead. Mount Shasta, a gigantic, white cone. The permanent snows hugging its sides looked like layers of ice cream. If the mountain erupted, all that snow would be instantly transformed into muddy slush, which would slide off and smother the valleys below.

The rest of the flight was a smooth glide to the southern base of Shasta, where a small town, a huddle of pine buildings, sat on the slope a mile or two below the tree line.

Garsprinilla swooped over McCloud like an airliner. Her passengers gazed down. The place looked deserted: not a soul, not a wagon moved on its streets. No horses stood tethered to hitching posts. Beyond the town limits lay forest and more forest, but there was a clearing about a mile away. Toward the near end of it sat a clutch of wigwams surrounded by a ring of totem poles.

North turned and said, "Shasta tribe."

Garsprinilla chose the far end of the clearing for her landing, which she executed flawlessly. After running a few short steps, she lowered her body to the ground and grunted.

"Egads, I'm tired. Wasn't cut out to be a beast of burden. All right, you hairless monkeys, climb off, so I can get back to civilization."

The passengers debarked.

Morrolan began, "If there is ever anything we can we do to repay this kindness.—"

Garsprinilla fixed him with a withering stare. "What did you have in mind?"

Morrolan stammered a noncommittal reply, but Garsprinilla was already loping away, going into her takeoff run.

"Thank you!" Marianne yelled, waving. She thought someone should say something.

Garsprinilla suddenly stopped, arched her back, and without further preamble, summarily vented a thunderous fart.

"Oh, dear," Marianne said. "I hope that's not a comment."

"I'm afraid it is," Morrolan said. "Greats are a touchy bunch. I wonder what Orifex is blackmailing her with."

After watching the dragon lift majestically into the air, the four passengers began to walk back across the clearing.

"You said these are Shasta?" Tom asked, pointing to the wigwams.

"Right," North said. "Nothing to worry about. The native populations here are generally pacific. Have been since the Europeans came to California."

"There they are."

A group of Indians stood watching, their faces and postures conveying only an intense, silent curiosity. The whole tribe had turned out. Men, women, and children, variously dressed in native costumes of deerskin and fur, observed the progress of the white strangers through the clearing.

"Perhaps they've never seen anyone ride a dragon before?" Tom ventured.

"Maybe," Morrolan said. "I sense, though, that they're interested in us for other reasons. Just what, I couldn't say."

"Morrolan," Tom said, "have you given any thought to a way we can fight automatons? Muscle doesn't work, and neither do guns, I'm thinking."

"I've given it some thought," Morrolan said. "Guns will work, with the right bullets."

"Silver, maybe?"

"Silver bullets. Hmmm. No, actually, I was thinking more of iron."

"Meteoric iron?" Marianne asked.

"If we had the iron," Tom said, "and if we had a shot mold, we'd have iron shot."

"If we had the iron," Marianne added.

Tom grinned at her. "If we had cap-and-ball firearms, which we don't." He pulled out his Colt .45 Peacemaker and cocked it.

North withdrew his pistol. "This is a converted percussion weapon. I guess a gunsmith could revert it. And as far as getting iron bullets, hell, any gunsmith ought to have a bullet matrix."

"He'll have to have a furnace hot enough to melt iron," Tom said.

"If we had a gunsmith," Marianne said.

"I do believe I saw a shot tower as we passed over the town," North said. "An old one, probably not in use. A town this isolated is bound to've made their own shot, back in the Gold Rush days."

"But how do we get meteoritic iron?" Tom asked. "Wait for a meteor to drop from the sky?"

"'Meteorite' is the word," Morrolan said. "Essentially, yes, we wait for a meteorite to drop."

Tom gave Morrolan a long look. "You're not joshing, are you?"

"You can cast a spell to summon just about anything. Meteorites are no exception. I've done it once, in fact, just for the thrill. Tricky thing, though. We'd have to go a ways out of town, for safety. It's usually a military spell."

"Military?"

"You'll see why," Morrolan said, "if it works."

McCloud now seemed not entirely lifeless. There were two horses tethered outside the saloon. Better yet, tinkling piano music came from within.

"Clint Eastwood movie," Tom said, looking up and down the street. It did look for all the world like a movie set.

"Eh?" North said.

Tom gave him a shrug. "Let's try the saloon."

"I could use a drink."

"D'you think they serve gin?" Morrolan said.

"Don't know, Ruggles. We'll see."

Fourteen

HE SALOON CONTINUED the movie theme. Everything was in place: big mirror behind the bar, bright brass fixtures, tables covered in green felt. A grand staircase led up to a gallery crossing the room, thence to rooms on the second floor. The piano was playing by itself.

"What'll it be, gentlemen?" the bald, mustachioed bartender said. He bowed slightly toward Marianne. "Ma'am." He looked human enough, Tom thought.

So did the two grizzled prospector types sitting at a table near the bar. They were eyeing the strangers with sullen interest.

"Do you have brandy?" Marianne said.

The bartender laughed. "Ma'am, same bottle of brandy's been behind the bar since the place opened. I reckon we do have some."

"Good, it's aged."

"That it is, ma'am."

"I'll have whiskey," Tom said.

"Gin and tonic, please," Morrolan said.

"No gin, sir."

"Blast."

North ordered whiskey, too.

"Fancy piano you got, there," Tom said.

The bartender poured Tom a shot. "Never could keep a piano player around long enough. Got plugged, most of 'em. So I had this mechanical gizmo freighted up from Sacramento. Cost a mint, but people come from miles around on a Saturday night just to feed pennies into that thing and hear it bat out a tune. . . ." The bartender's face fell. "Used to, anyway." He turned away and fiddled with something behind the bar.

Tom downed his shot. It was pure rotgut, but he stifled a gasp successfully. "Rough stuff."

"Ran through the good stock, sir. Sorry about that," the bartender said with his back still turned. "Haven't been able to order anything new for some time."

"Oh? Why?"

"One thing or another," was all the bartender had to reply.

"Whiskey here's good enough for me," came a voice from the table.

The strangers turned.

"Gentlemen," Tom said. "Good day."

One of the men was tall and rangy, the other a rounded sort with small eyes. Both were bearded. The tall one's grin exposed a long picket-row of yellow teeth. "Now what the hell kind of monkey suit is that, mister?"

He was addressing Morrolan, who looked down at his typically English outfit. To his mind, it wasn't so much a monkey suit as a proper attire. "Like this ascot?" he said.

"And that hat sure does look pretty," the small-eyed one said. "Why, I'm surprised the lady don't wear it."

"This, my dear fellows, is a riding hat."

The two men howled. Wiping tears away, the rounded one burbled, "Did y'ever hear such fancy talk, Reuben? 'My dear fellows.'"

Reuben and his friend continued to trade impressions of Morrolan for some time before at last subsiding.

"Mind if I ask a question?" Tom said.

"Fire away, mister," the tall one said.

"Is there a good gunsmith in town?"

"You look well-heeled. What for you need a gunsmith?"

"Some repairs. Know of a good one?"

"One right up the street," the bartender said. "Emil Bass, by name. Bass Gun Emporium."

"He have a shot mold?"

"Shot mold? Oh. Yeah, I would expect so."

"Now, what the hell would you city folks want with a shot mold?" the beady-eyed prospector said, almost accusingly.

"We collect antique weapons," Tom said. "Have a need for shot. You have a problem with that?"

"Why, damnedest fool thing I ever heard," the man said, reaching for his side arm. "What's the use of a—"

Marianne's Colt Navy revolver was out, cocked, and pointed before the man's gun had cleared the holster. Tom and North had only reached for their side arms.

"—lead ball when you got . . . cartridges. . . ." The small eyes became grew larger as the man collapsed internally. Slowly, his gun drooped back into the holster.

Reuben displayed his horse teeth again. "Ain't they a bunch of citified pansies. Havin' their woman protect 'em."

"She's usually the fastest," Tom said. "And she's a crack shot, too. Care to try her?"

"Mighty jumpy, aren't you, stranger?" the rangy one said. "Cal here, he weren't intendin' anything."

Tom's attention was diverted the slightest bit by more men coming into the saloon. He didn't like the looks of them.

"Your friend ought to know better than to draw his weapon in a place like this," Tom said, taking his hand off his pistol grip.

Marianne turned once completely about. When she faced away from the bar again, her weapon had retreated to the place whence it had come.

"Didn't mean nothin' by it," Cal grumbled.

"We couldn't take the chance," Marianne said. "Just remember that the next time you feel the need to draw your weapons."

"Lady," the rangy one said, "you got more brass than a St. Louis fire engine. Gotta give you that."

Marianne turned around and drank her brandy. It had been served in a proper snifter, which she hadn't expected.

"Any trouble?" a newcomer demanded of Tom. He was a broad-shouldered man in a deerskin jacket, boots, and wide hat.

"No trouble," Tom said, "just a little misunderstanding. You the law around here, mister?"

The man smiled, showing discolored teeth. "Name's Tilley. Evan Tilley. No law here, mister. Imperial constable stops in about every month, asks around if anything's doin'. Other than that, we're pretty much on our own up here. Nothing to do but logging, or a little ranching, or maybe a little prospecting. Mind if I ask what you folks are doing in these parts?"

"We're geologists," Tom said, going with the agreed cover story. "From the United States. We're here to observe Mount Shasta. We've recorded some seismic disturbances that we think are coming from the mountain. We're worried it might erupt."

"Now what's the United States got to worry about? Mountain's a thousand miles away from any U.S. territory. This here's the republic of California, mister."

"Our two governments are cooperating," Tom said. "You people out here don't have much in the way of trained geologists."

"Not so, mister. We got the best in California, though we don't got any fancy titles after our names. You can't prospect if you don't know your rocks and soils and such."

Tom nodded. "True, but science has something to contribute."

"Maybe so," the man said. "As to that mountain up there, we don't set much store by it, though the redskins do. They tell all kinds of stories about it.

For us, it's just a mountain. It may pass a little gas from time to time, but there's not a man in this town ever pays it any mind."

While talking, Tom had been sizing up the tactical situation. About ten men had entered the bar and taken seats in various locations. If it came to a shoot-out, Tom and company were outflanked and outgunned.

But it didn't look to be coming to a shoot-out, leastwise not at the moment. Good thing.

"One more thing," Tom said. "If you could direct us to the general store, we'd be appreciative."

"Just down the street. You intend on doing some mountain climbing?"

"Perhaps. We might have to take readings at higher altitudes."

The man shook his head. "You oughtn't to go up there, mister. You run into one of them gas clouds, it'll choke you to death."

"We're fully trained to handle the dangers of vulcanology, sir, but thanks just the same." Tom tossed a coin on the bar. "Have a drink on me."

The man smiled again, showing more bad teeth. What this town needs is a good dentist, Tom thought.

"Why, thank you kindly, sir."

"Damnedest gee-ologists I ever seen," Reuben muttered. "One dressed like a dandy, woman packs a pistol, them other two come in here armed to the teeth, orderin' people around. . . ." He continued airing grievances in this vein until the four strangers left the saloon.

The general store, just a few doors away, was closed. Thick dust on the goods in the display window was evidence that it had been closed for some time. Despite this, the place looked to be well-stocked.

"Don't see any climbing gear," Tom said. "Maybe we can get rope somewhere else, and the blacksmith to make us some pitons."

"Let's just break in," North said, "take what we need, and leave some cash."

Tom inclined his head back toward the saloon. "Tilley and his men might object, unless we're good burglars."

"I'm a fair burglar," North said.

"Then we'll give it a try. Dust in the place is pretty thick. Owner must've left months ago."

"I wonder what the townspeople do for supplies," Marianne said.

"What did you make of Cal and Reuben?" North said.

"Funny enough, they may be OK," Tom said. "Drifted in, maybe."

"If I hadn't been so trigger-happy," Marianne said, "perhaps we could have persuaded them to help us."

"You did the right thing, Marianne," Morrolan said.

"But we might need some help," Tom said. "Let's go see Mr. Bass and his emporium."

Bass Gun Emporium was not shut, but no one was behind the counter. The four stood around looking at various firearms until a portly, bespectacled man exited from behind a curtain at the back of the store.

"Can I help you folks?"

"Mr. Bass?"

"That's the name."

"Mr. Bass, do you do bullet casting?"

"I have plenty of ammunition. What caliber to you need?"

"We have a special need, and it's rather unusual. We need bullets made of iron."

The man squinted one eye. "Iron. Why, that's . . . that is unusual. Whatever for?"

"Hard to explain. Can you do it for us?"

"Iron bullets? Mister, if you don't mind my saying so, that's the craziest thing I've ever heard. Why . . . first off, I'm not set up to melt iron. Lead has a very low melting temperature, you know."

"I know. Look if you can't do bullets, perhaps you could use your shot mold to . . ."

"Why, that hasn't been used for ten years. Grate's all rusted out up top. Second thing, cast-iron bullets, or shot . . . why, they'll shatter to bits when they hit. That's the nastiest thing I ever heard. There's no call to hurt people more than you have to, is there?"

"It's not people we're after," Tom said. "Look—"

"What you want is steel. Steel bullets or steel-jacketed. I heard of them, but people got no use for them in these parts."

"They wouldn't do us any good. Is the blacksmith open today?"

Bass shook his head. "Jim Riley closed up his smithy three months ago and lighted off for Portland. And if I didn't have a sick wife upstairs, I'd have done the same. This town ain't fit for people no more."

"Tilley and his men take it over?"

Bass eyed his customers up and down. "You're strangers. Listen mister, if I were you, I'd give this town a wide berth. In fact, I wouldn't come within fifty miles of this town or that mountain up there."

"What's been happening?"

Bass shook his head again. "You'd say I was crazy."

"Try us."

"Strange doings," Bass said. "Passing strange. This used to be a fine place to live. Then Tilley and his gang moved in, and it hasn't been the same since. Besides. . . ."

"What else?"

"Like I said, you'd never believe it. I don't half believe it myself. Something happened to people. Not everybody, just here and there. People started acting different than the way they used to. Not normal. Not anything you could put your finger on, either. Just . . . not right. My son-in-law, for instance. My daughter says he came home one night from his silver mine, and he was changed. Changed, that's all. She couldn't even put it into words. That's been happening all over. People are frightened. Most of 'em moved away. McCloud's a ghost town now. I spend every day scared out of my wits. It's that mountain. . . ." Bass turned and looked off toward the back of the store. "That infernal mountain. Something's got into it. Something bad." He brought his gaze slowly around to his customers again. "Evil."

Tom placed a hand on Bass's shoulder. "Mr. Bass, we know just what you mean."

Bass frowned. "You do? Are you from the government?"

"The government may be in on it," Tom said. "But we're here to see what we can do about getting rid of Tilley, his men, and maybe what's up in that mountain. That's why we need your help. Are you willing?"

Bass broke out into a smile that radiated hope and relief. "Mister, are you on the level?"

"Trust us."

"I will. Mister, you're the first ray of sunshine I've seen in these parts for more than a year. I'll do everything I can. I'll cast those bullets for you. I'll carve 'em if I have to."

"Good. We're going to book rooms in the hotel— if that's open for business."

"It is, Mister . . ."

"Olam. Thomas Olam. Think we'll have any trouble there?"

"Ettie Wong runs the hotel. Chinese woman, but she's Christian. As hard-bitten a gal as you'll ever run across. Nothing could make her leave town. She says she'll see this thing through."

"Well," Tom said, "we'll go see Ettie Wong. Then we'll come back to discuss business with you."

"I'll start seeing what I can do about the iron."

"We'll supply the iron. It can't be any iron. We need something special."

"What kind of special?"

"Meteor iron."

"Oh. What the Faerie folk call cold iron?"

"Exactly."

Fifteen

STANDING IN AN alpine meadow on the slope of the mountain, Tom looked up at the night sky. "How long do you think it'll take?"

Morrolan was looking too. The bowl of night was an endless cosmos of a million stars, and hovering just on the edge of perceptibility, intermixed with their brighter cousins, a million more. Starlight glistened on the mountain's snows, high above.

"Don't know, really. On any given evening, a fair number of falling stars appear. But we need one big enough to survive the fall, yet small enough to avoid smashing us, the town, and most of the county. If they have counties here."

"Yeah, it'd be nice to avoid all that," Tom said. "Think you can do it?"

"What, avoid calling down a boulder the size of that mountain? Quite easily. What's more likely to happen is that the meteorite will be consumed before hitting the earth."

"A cinder's not going to do us any good," Tom said.

"Nor is a lump of nickel-iron—that's what these bits are usually composed of—the size of a city block. T'would be a trifle clumsy to haul around, eh?"

"Yup."

Morrolan smiled. "Yup? You know, Thomas, you're really fitting into this Western ambience."

"He does ride rather tall in the saddle," Marianne said, giving Tom's left buttock a squeeze.

"Ouch. Careful, I'm a little sore in that area."

North was scanning the sky, as well. "Frankly, I've never trusted magic. Sorry, I'm still skeptical."

Morrolan waved it aside. "No need to apologize. Magic isn't the most reliable thing in the world. But it does work. And . . . well . . . hmmmm . . ."

Marianne pointed skyward. "Look!"

"A shooting star," North said. "But it's not moving."

"It is," Morrolan said. "In fact, it's coming toward us."

"I'll be damned."

"Just hope you won't be dashed."

The horse harnessed to Ettie Wong's buckboard began to whinny and stamp its feet.

"Getting brighter, nearer," Morrolan said.

"Should we take cover?" North asked worriedly.

"It looks as though it's going to weigh about two hundred stone. No cover against that. It would crash through the trees, or any roof for that matter."

"How can you tell how big it is?"

"You develop an eye for these things."

The star grew bright enough to hurt the eyes before it whooshed overhead, trailing a stream of smoke and making a sound like a rushing locomotive. It hit the meadow with a dull thud. The horse, neighing piteously, would have bolted had Tom not been holding it by the bridle.

Then a glowing bit of something bounced high into the air and rocketed into the trees.

That was the entire show, save for a burning smell riding the night breeze, and the smoke rising skyward. They all ran for the trees.

They found the thing sizzling in the damp undergrowth a few feet from a narrow stream that cut through the meadow. It was a twisted, pitted mass of red-hot metal the size of a bed pillow.

"Perfect!" Morrolan said triumphantly.

"There's our iron," Tom said, with some satisfaction. "Well done, Morrolan."

"Thank you, sir."

"But we have to let it cool before we move it, and then we have to melt it again. Going to be hard."

"We won't have to melt it at all," Morrolan said.

"No? But what are we—"

"Leave it to me and Mr. Bass," Morrolan said.

"How long to cool?" Tom asked.

"We should leave it overnight."

Tom looked around. "I don't like that."

"Then let's quench it in the brook."

"Grab a stick."

They found sticks and levered the thing up onto a wider end, then pushed it over. In this wise, they rolled it into the water, where it hissed and howled and threw up a column of steam.

"We're making enough noise, aren't we?" Tom said.

"I'll bring the wagon down," Marianne said, and exited the woods.

Presently, the lump of sky-metal quieted down, content to boil the water. In a short time, the cool mountain stream rendered it into a lump of warm iron, which Tom and North then hauled out of the water and set on the ground.

"Heavy bugger," North said with a grunt.

Morrolan stooped to inspect it. "Can't see much, but it looks fine for the purpose. Now, we must get it back to Mr. Bass's."

Marianne drove the wagon up, and the men loaded the meteorite into the wagon bed. They had nothing to stop it from rattling around loose, so North sat in the wagon with his feet bracing it against the side. Making do with these half measures and wishing he'd thought of bringing ropes or straps, Tom giddapped the horse back in the direction of town, Marianne riding shotgun, Morrolan following with the other horses.

About halfway back to town, moving shadows bunched up ahead on the trail. A struck match first illuminated a man on horseback, then the miner's lantern he held. His companions were Tilley and most of his men. The lantern was the type that threw light forward, illuminating the wagon but not many of the reception committee.

The rest of the gang were probably in the weeds with rifles, Tom surmised.

"Now, you people've been up to some mighty strange things since you got here," Tilley said.

"Such as?" Tom said as the horse came to a stop.

"Running around out here at all hours of the night. People heard some strange noises a while back. What've you got there in that wagon?"

"A scientific specimen. Meteor."

"Meteor?"

"Falling star. We were making some astronomical observations when it fell to earth very near here. We're just lucky, I guess. We're taking it back to examine it. Science, you know."

"Yeah. Well, your doings have been upsetting people in these parts."

"We just got here, Tilley," Tom said. "Haven't had near enough time to upset anyone."

"Well, you got me all flustered to hell."

Tilley's men guffawed with him.

"You come here, looking like some kind of Yankee gunslingers, with a woman who wears men's pants and draws quicker than a man. You come out here with this English pansy in the middle of the night, and he starts chantin' like some kind of faerie high priest—"

"You were spying on us," Tom said.

"You can't do much in this town I don't know about," Tilley said with smug pride.

"You run McCloud, do you?"

"That's right. And you're not going back there, ever. You're coming with us."

"Sorry, we have business back in town."

The sound of many firing pins clicking back sounded like crickets in the night.

With a broad grin, Tilley drew his gun slowly. "Like I said, you're coming with us. Back up that mountain."

"Is that where you're taking orders from?"

"Never you mind. Just turn this wagon around."

"Not enough room for that, Tilley."

"Gets wider just down the road a ways. Pull her forward, easy now. Remember, we got you covered."

"Boss . . ." one of Tilley's men asked.

"I wouldn't advise you try any funny stuff. I know you people got tricks up your sleeves."

"Boss . . . Boss?"

"What is it?" Tilley said irritably.

"Boss, look up there."

"Look up where?"

"The sky, Boss."

"What the hell are you talkin' about?"

Another shooting star was blossoming overhead, this one immensely brighter, burning with a green, malevolent light.

"What is that?"

"Look at it!"

"What's going on?" Tilley demanded.

"My fault, I'm afraid," Morrolan said. "Sorry about that, but I seem to have overdone the meteor-summoning spell."

Straining to see Morrolan in the darkness, Tilley said, "What the hell is he jabberin' about?"

"Well, I'm only a pansy Englishman, but I cast a good spell, and this time I've done it too good by half. That thing up there is a very large meteor, sized about as big as an average house. And it is headed this way. It will strike in my vicinity. So, I suggest that everyone disperse while I stay here. I can protect myself, but none of you."

Taking advantage of the distraction, Marianne had furtively drawn her gun. Firing from the hip, she took out the lantern in one shot.

Yee-haaaah! Tom yelled, and the horse bolted forward. The night erupted in pandemonium, gunfire coming from all directions.

Bullets whizzed past Tom and Marianne as the buckboard rolled headlong down the twisting mountain trail, the horse running away at a panicked gallop. Tom strained to rein it back into a safer gate, but failed. The wagon tilted up at the next turn, and Tom and Marianne had to cantilever themselves over the side like the crew of a jibing racing yacht to keep it from overturning. Shadows hid the next bend, which threatened to be even worse than the last, but Tom and Marianne were prepared for it . . . when the thing from the sky struck.

The impact was directly behind them. There was a blinding burst of light, the sound of thunder, then a shock wave that swept the wagon over the edge of the trail.

Tom found himself rolling down the hill through the underbrush, the wagon tumbling and crashing close behind him, flying into splinters. He rolled and rolled and rolled, without being able to stop. The slope was terrifyingly steep, and he was torn between wanting to stop, for fear of tumbling over a shear cliff, and not wanting to stop, for fear of being crushed by the wagon. For the briefest fraction of a second, he glimpsed Marianne flying over him, disappearing into the flame-lit murk, chased by a loose wagon wheel.-

His memory, like a tape recording arbitrarily cut, ended there.

Sixteen

FULL CONSCIOUSNESS CAME slowly. He was surrounded by greenery, through which leaked a liquid sunlight. He tried to sit up, but a bolt of pain through his back made him writhe. He tried again, gritting through the pain. Weeds clawed at his face. He spat out dirt.

He didn't know where he was, and had only a dim notion of who he was. There was only one thought in his mind.

Marianne.

She was important above all. He had to know where Marianne was. Who was Marianne? She was the woman he loved. That's all he needed to know.

Weeds, grass, fronds, everything impeded his progress. Branches snagged at him, preventing him from coming into full daylight. Living things tugged at him, calling him back to rest and oblivion. He told them no.

He clawed his way along the ground, hurting and aching. Finally, he found there was nothing preventing him from standing up, so he decided to try it.

He made it. He was standing on a slope. Below lay the bottom of a gully, a jumble of shattered wood and loose wheels in the middle of it. A wagon. A crashed wagon. A buckboard, from the look of it. Had he anything to do with it? Or had the wreck been there some time?

He ambled down the slope and looked through the debris. All he knew or cared about was that Marianne was not there. He had to find her.

Why?

He didn't know for sure, but the need was great. However, there was nothing in the vicinity useful as a clue to her whereabouts. He was very sad about that, and he cried for a short time. Then he decided to stop crying.

Someone was looking at him, watching him. He twirled about, eyes searching the hillsides, but nobody showed himself. No sign of anyone.

He heard, or thought he heard, someone chuckling.

No, no one around.

He began to climb out of the gully but was stopped by the sight of a severed human arm, still wrapped in a torn shirtsleeve.

He stooped and examined it, and was relieved to find a male hand at the end of it. But something curious about the shoulder caught his attention. He moved the thing for a better look. Protruding from the torn sleeve was not bone or sinew, but—was it possible?—metal. Wires, cables, wheels, and gears. He picked the thing up. It was not a human arm after all, but a part of a doll or dummy. A manikin? He didn't know. He threw the thing aside and climbed out of the gully.

Halfway up the slope, he found a gun, a revolver, and it was familiar. It read COLT on the barrel, and there were five cartridges in the cylinder.

His hand went to his side. He was wearing a holster. An empty holster. The Colt fit nicely into it, as if it were used to the worn leather pocket.

He saw something strange at the top of the hill. Many trees were down, laid out in a circular pattern with the center about a hundred yards up the road. Curious. But he didn't feel compelled to investigate.

The walk down the mountain road was enjoyable, and the fresh mountain air cleared his head. If only this walk could continue forever, he thought.

But his driving need was still finding Marianne. He had to know what had happened to her.

He came to a town, and it looked strangely familiar. Yes, he'd been here before. What was the name of the town? He didn't know. He walked down the main street, looking, wondering.

The streets were deserted. As he turned a corner, he heard the tinkle of piano music, and it drew him onward, up steps and onto the plank sidewalk, past storefronts, and through swinging doors into a big saloon. This looked familiar, too.

Men, about ten or twelve of them, sat at tables, drinking and playing cards. He looked toward the source of the music. No one was playing the piano.

His head began to hurt, and he sat down. No one looked at him, no one said anything.

After a long time, someone placed a glass in front of him.

"Can I pour you a drink, sir?"

He looked up. A bartender. His face was familiar.

"Drink, sir?"

He nodded. The man poured him some whiskey and went away.

He drank the whiskey. He didn't taste it at all, but it felt good going into him. It crashed into his stomach and sent waves of warmth through him. Gradually, his surroundings began to take on some meaning. The saloon. Tilley's men. Tilley . . .

He got up, searched the room, saw Evan Tilley, and walked over to him.

"Where is she?"

Tilley looked up from his poker hand. "Uh . . . you talkin' to me?"

"What have you done with Marianne?"

Tilley shrugged. "Sir, I don't believe I've had the pleasure of makin' your acquaintance." He dropped a coin into the pile of money at the center of the table. "I call."

"I said, what have you done with her? Tell me, or I'll kill you."

Tilley slowly stood up. "Mister, I don't know who you are, or what your business is, or what the hell you think you're doing talkin' to me that way, but I'm standin' here to tell you that I ain't ever laid eyes on you before, and that if you want trouble, that's exactly what you're going to get."

"What's the ruckus here?" came a voice at his back.

Tilley pointed a finger. "This critter comes walkin' in and accuses me of messin' with his woman, by the name of Mary Anne or whatever the hell. Now, you tell him to back on out or get his face shot off."

"No need for that. Mister . . . I say, mister?"

He turned. It was the bartender, brandishing a shotgun. "What you need is another drink to calm you down. Otherwise, you'll get a taste of buckshot. Now, come along here and don't start no trouble."

"He took Marianne."

"We'll find her. Why, what you ought to do is talk to the imperial constable. That's what. He'll be in town in about two days, so it's only a matter of waitin'—"

Tom brushed past the bartender and strode out the door.

The street was still deserted. The sun was low, shadows were long. He couldn't understand this because he had just gotten up. Hadn't he? What had happened to the day? Unless . . .

He staggered along the sidewalk, his head smarting fiercely. He had been knocked out, that's what the trouble was. He had been unconscious for a long while. How long? Maybe a night and a day. Maybe two days. Marianne . . . Morrolan! Where the hell was Morrolan? And . . . another man. Who?

He passed a shop that put him in mind of a shop he'd seen before. Bass Gun Emporium, the lettering on the window read. The door was open, so he went in.

The man behind the counter took no notice of his entry.

"Mr. Bass?"

"Yes?"

"Mr. Bass, it's me . . . it's . . ."

"Yes, sir? Have we met?"

"We talked yester—before. Sometime."

"Sorry, mister. I don't recall. What'd you say your name was?"

"I don't know."

"You say you don't know your own name?"

"I can't remember. A lot of things . . . are fuzzy. "

"Mister, you must've got hold of some bad liquor. It can do that to you. I suggest you go somewhere and sleep it off, then you'll get a better grip on things. Now if you'll excuse me, I got work to do."

Bass exited through a curtain covering a door at the back, and was gone.

Tom left the shop and continued to roam the streets, trying to focus the cloud of uncertainty that seemed to hang above his head. There was a lot in that cloud, a lot of information, and if he could just coalesce it, condense it, have it rain down on him in an ablution of truth and certainty, then everything would be all right. As it was, he simply walked aimlessly from building to building.

Hotel. He went in. A young Oriental man behind the desk smiled pleasantly.

"Do I have a room here?"

The young man frowned. "Yes?"

"Do I have a room at his hotel? I think I checked into this hotel. Is there a room for me?"

"You want room? We have room."

"No. I have a room. I think. Don't I?"

The young man shrugged. "We have room. You want room? You sign." He pushed a registration book forward.

"No. Listen. I think I already have a room at this hotel. I'm sick, and I can't remember. Help me, please."

The man raised his voice and spoke something in Chinese. An Oriental woman, about fifty, came out of an office behind the desk.

"May I help you?"

"I hope so. I'm sick, I was hurt. I hurt my head, and I want to know if I have a room at this hotel."

"I'm sorry, sir, I don't think so. We do have vacant rooms. Plenty of them. Would you like to book a room to stay in?"

"I have to find Marianne. I know I've met you before. I remember your face. Have you seen the woman I was with? Her name is Marianne."

The woman shook her head. "I'm sorry, sir. I'm quite sure I've never seen you before, and I've never met the lady. Good day."

Back out to the deserted streets. Didn't anyone live in this town? He hadn't seen a horse or a wagon.

Wagon. The crashed wagon. He had been driving it. Last night, or whenever it was. Something had happened. A blinding explosion, a tremendous impact . . . something. And the wagon had gone off the road, down the slope. Marianne had been with him! Yes, now he remembered.

There was a man standing in the middle of the street, holding a gun. The gun barked, and a bullet sang past.

Acting on instinct, Tom drew and fired, and was astonished to see his bullet hit its mark, puffing the cloth of the man's shirt. But the hit had no effect. The man fired again.

Tom felt a burning sensation in his left shoulder. Stepping backward, he got off another shot, and again he saw that he was dead on. Once more, the man shot at him.

Tom ducked into an alley and ran its length, coming out into another street. Suddenly, the dirt on the street fountained up as he heard a rifle report at his back. He whirled and fired upward. The man who held the rifle, kneeling on a rooftop, laughed at him.

Tom fired again. Another laugh, with a rifle shot to back it up. He dove behind a water trough and crawled, multiple shots plunking into the water as he moved.

He peeked out from behind and searched the rooftops. How many were there?

Fire from three different directions came at him, and he thought it was about time to move to a different street.

He jumped up and ran, firing off a shot wildly. He crashed through a door and made his way through what appeared to be a laundry. Rushing through a back room full of tubs and hanging clothes, he came out into the front room, vaulted the counter, and moved to the door, which he cracked and looked through. No sign of the first man with whom he'd exchanged leaden gifts.

He touched his shoulder and came away with blood. Drawing his coat down, he examined himself. Just a graze, a little deep, but nothing serious. The wound was oozing a bit, but there was nothing to do for it.

Before he left the laundry, he reloaded his pistol. He was down to three spare cartridges. He'd have to make every shot count.

The gunfighting had cleared his head somewhat, dispersing that fuzzy cloud over him and filling him with a resolve to achieve a definite though limited goal: to find out who was doing the shooting and stop them. He hadn't forgotten about Marianne and the task of finding her, but this small job had a more pressing priority.

He exited the laundry, turning left. At once, a volley of shots came at him, and he sought refuge behind a pile of crates. Sprays of wood splinters hit him in the face each time he raised his head to look at his enemies. Glass shattered in the windows behind him. Most of the shots came from high above: more men on the rooftops.

By a combination dead reckoning and rough triangulation, he located the approximate positions of the snipers and decided to make a break for it across the street, back to the gun emporium, to find more ammunition. It was either that or stay here and be splintered to death.

He jumped up and raced over the street's packed dirt, bullets tracing his path, more outlining every way he could possibly twist, until he could not move.

They were just toying with him. They could kill him at any time, but they were having a bit of fun. He stood in the middle of the bullet-sprayed street, turning this way and that, trying to see who was shooting at him.

One by one, they obliged, standing up for him to take a shot.

"Here I am!"

"Come on, shoot me!"

"Over here, Easterner!"

They waved their rifles, laughing. He fired at each of them, taking careful aim, having all the time in the world. He hit all of them, and none of them fell. His bullets pinged off their chests, their faces, their stomachs.

They aren't men at all, he thought.

Robots! Automatons!

He remembered. He remembered almost everything now.

A bullet hissed by his ear. They were firing at him again, and this time, he thought, they meant to kill him.

He ran a zigzag to Bass's shop window and dove headfirst through it. Then he lay there among the broken glass, dazed, listening.

The shooting had stopped. All was quiet outside. He got up and searched the shop. But he didn't need to search long.

There, on the counter, was a box of bullets with a note, written in a strange runic script:

Tom,

> *Here are the special bullets you need. No lack of cold iron, with that second drop. No need to melt and do the shot mold business or the Martix, should have thought of it right off. Just iron fillings, easy enough. A spot of epoxy on a clump of the stuff, then hollow out regular bullets, tamp it in, there you go. Same effect. Use them in good health. Moriarty and I looked for you and Marianne last night. Where were you? You'll here from me.*

> *Morrolan*

"Moriarty?"

He stood there, reading the note over and over again. There were the cartridges, true enough, their blunt tips tampered with in some way. But where the hell had Moriarty come from? And how the hell had he connected up with Morrolan? Egads, he needed a few explanations.

The last missing piece of his memory fell into place. He and Moriarty had agreed to meet here in McCloud. And Moriarty had made good on his word. Easy enough to explain.

He reached into a secret pouch in the lining of his coat and brought out a small hand mirror. He peered into it, and spoke.

"Morrolan? Morrolan, come in."

The mirror remained a mirror. It seemed to have no desire to transform itself into a two-way walkie-talkie/TV. He put it back into his coat.

He loaded his gun with the new ammunition. The only place he knew in this town that could possibly serve up answers was the saloon. He aimed to go there and have it out with Tilley.

The cloud of uncertainty was gone. He knew who he was, where he was, and what had happened. But one thing had not changed.

He would find Marianne, or die.

Seventeen

TOM WAS WALKING back to the saloon when he met Sam Clemens coming the other way, still dressed in his characteristic white suit, still quietly puffing a cigar.

Tom stopped and regarded his approach. Clemens walked by, smiling pleasantly, leaving a fragrant trail of smoke.

"Good evening, sir," Clemens said.

"What do you know about all this?" Tom demanded of Clemens's back.

"I wouldn't go into that saloon," Clemens said. "Whiskey's terrible." Spoken like a ghost delivering a warning to mortal men.

Tom watched him turn a corner. When all this was over, he was going to have to sit down with that man and ask him how the hell he gets from one place to another. Maybe he *was* a ghost.

The awful, ever-present piano music—Tom hadn't recognized a single tune so far—seemed cranked up to deafening proportions. Or perhaps he had grown oversensitive to it.

He pushed through the swinging doors to find the place deserted save for Tilley himself, sitting at a far table, playing solitaire.

Tom crossed the floor slowly. "Tilley."

Tilley looked up. "Evenin'."

"Where is Marianne?"

Tilley cupped his ear. "What say?"

"I said, where is the woman?"

"Sorry, mister, can't hear you properly."

"I said—"

Tom drew his gun and fired at the piano. It died immediately with a rattle and a whine. A nervous silence fell.

"I said," Tom continued, "where is the woman?"

"Oh, well, she's upstairs. The boys are takin' turns with her. You know how boys are. They need their fun."

"Get up, Tilley."

"Hell, I just put up the fourth ace. I'm about to win this game."

"Get up, you miserable bastard! Or whatever you are."

Tilley threw down his cards and rose from the chair. "Mister, you don't learn your lessons too easy. We thought we taught you one out in that street. You can't hurt us, now, you know that. So what's the use of—"

Tom drew and shot him cleanly through the chest.

Tilley's smile faded to a perplexed frown. He bent his head and watched his fingers palpate the hole in his chest. A look of horror grew on his face. Clutching at his chest, he collapsed to his knees.

"The true death!" he screamed. "The true death!"

"You should have taken a cue from the piano."

"The true . . ." Tilley keeled over on his face and was still.

The bartender popped up behind the bar with a shotgun. Tom whirled and shot him. Both barrels went off toward the ceiling and took out the chandelier. The place went dark.

But light leaked from outside.

Tom mounted the staircase to the second story slowly. It wasn't long before a human form rushed out of the doorway at the far end of the landing that made a bridge across the first floor. Tom shot twice, and a man came tumbling down the steps. He stepped aside and kicked him by. He resumed climbing.

There was another blur of movement above, this time with gunfire attached. Bullets chewed up the woodwork beside Tom's head as he fired upward. The gunman—rather, another mechanical simulacrum—went cartwheeling over the rail in classic fashion and crashed to the floor.

Tom got to the landing without further incident. But now he had to get through the arched doorway that led to the hall. This he did successfully, but then faced a long line of doors. A far one cracked open and emitted a burst of flame.

The bullet rasped by, missing his head by inches. He fired, and the door flew open as the gunman behind it fell into the hall.

He proceeded to repeat this video-game action for the nine remaining doors, dodging bullets at every step. Before long, robot-bodies littered the passageway. When the last gunman had been vanquished, he checked all the rooms. No Marianne.

He heard a chuckle again. Where? Behind him, or in one of the rooms?

"Tom!"

Marianne's voice! From downstairs.

He ran back down the hallway, vaulting over the bodies. When he came out onto the landing, he saw Marianne and North below, looking up at him.

"Marianne!"

"Tom, we thought you were dead."

"I thought you were dead. Where the hell have you been?"

He flew down the steps and into her arms. He kissed her resoundingly.

"We looked for you last night," Marianne said. "But we couldn't find you. Why are you looking at me so strangely?"

"Can't believe you're OK. I was out cold, in a tangle of bushes. Jeez, it's good to see you again. I've been looking all over town. It's full of automatons."

"We know," North said, shaking hands with Tom. "We found the entrance to the caves in the mountain."

"Where's Morrolan?"

"He's up there," Marianne said. "Come on, we have a carriage outside."

As North and Marianne moved toward the door, Tom asked, "What about Moriarty?"

"Moriarty?" They both halted.

"Yes, didn't Morrolan say anything about Moriarty?"

Marianne and North looked at each other. "No, he didn't say anything to us. Is Moriarty here?"

"I got a note from Morrolan. He must have told you about that. The magic bullets?"

"We know about them. They seem to work fine," Marianne said, looking down at Tilley.

"I still have some," Tom said. "We'll have to use them sparingly."

"Come on," North said. "No time to lose. Morrolan says he's got the big doors guarding the place figured out."

"Right, let's go," Tom said, following them out the swinging doors.

A horse and buggy waited in front. The three climbed aboard, North taking the reins.

"I think most of Tilley's men must have died in the big meteor strike last night," Tom said.

"We found lots of bodies," Marianne said.

"Today, they were replaced by automatons. I think Ettie Wong was, too. And Mr. Bass. Have you seen the real one?"

"He's at the mountain, too."

"Everybody must be up there."

North drove the buggy quickly out of town and up the mountain road. Above, in the late afternoon sun, Shasta looked like a titanic ice cream sundae, dabbed with caramel sauce and dotted with chocolate sprinkles.

About three miles up the slope, the road diverged, and North took the right fork, following a narrow, twisting trail through scraggly pine. It appeared to lead all the way up to the tree line, above which a bleak and barren band of volcanic ash swept up sharply to the lower edge of the glaciers.

But North did not drive all the way up to the tree line, instead taking yet another side road that wound through tremendous boulders, lava trees, and piles of pumice, interspersed with pines whose stature decreased with every foot of altitude.

They came to a wide, oval-shaped apron of filled earth that formed a table-like ledge on the side of the mountain. The carriage finally stopped in front of an impressive array of rocks set into the slope. These proceeded to move of their own accord, swinging out as if on gimbals to reveal the mouth of an immense cave with an interior as big as an airplane hangar. And indeed, airships—auto-gyros, their wings and rotors folded up—were harbored within. Two of them. Tom saw that there was room for a third.

"Morrolan's working overtime," North said.

"Pretty slick," Tom commented. "So this is Primus's hideout?"

"Yes," Marianne said. "Primus's base of operations."

"And it just opens up for us, like that," Tom said, drawing his gun.

"Morrolan can do anything," North said.

"Tom, what are you doing?"

Tom calmly shot North in the back and watched him fall out of the carriage.

"Tom! You shouldn't have done that!"

Tom got out and rolled the body over. The eyes were sightless and dead. Death had been instant, far quicker than the real North would have died.

"He's not North," Tom said. "He's a robot, has been all along. He's been spying for Primus. I don't know when they switched him, probably back at the hotel, maybe before. But now we—"

Tom turned and froze. Marianne was standing in the carriage, holding a gun on him.

"I wasn't sure," Tom said, dropping his gun and raising his hands. "I guess I didn't want to believe it."

"I shouldn't have kissed you," Marianne said. "They usually find out that way. Very difficult to simulate a human kiss. You should have shot me when you had the chance."

"I'm not sure I could have done it. Where's the real Marianne?"

The automaton that looked like Marianne inclined her head toward the cave. "In there. She's safe, don't worry. Primus does not lightly take human life."

"No, he—or should I say it—just wants to control human life."

"For the good of humankind," the automaton said. "Now, let's go in. You've had a long and arduous journey to reach this goal. It's time you were rewarded for your valiant efforts."

"One question, first. Back at the Palace, I could pretty much tell the automatons from the humans. Why did I miss with North? And with you for a moment at least."

"North and I are of the Star line of remote units. New improvements developed by Primus. Sam Clemens was the first, in fact."

"The manufacturing plant is at the hotel?"

"One of many all over the world," Marianne's double said.

"So Clemens and most government officials have been replicated?"

"With Kit Carson and all the rest, including the emperor."

"Of course. Well, shall we go in?"

Marianne's mechanical duplicate jumped down from the carriage. It seemed quite as nimble as the original.

"You know," Tom said, "you could take some kissing lessons from your real counterpart. She's an excellent kisser."

"I'm afraid sexual relations will be quite different under the new world order," the doppelgänger said. "In fact, there will be less emotion generally."

"I'm sure. Starting with happiness."

"It's overrated. Move ahead, please."

Eighteen

THE HANGAR AREA was even roomier than it looked from the outside, its ceiling a vault of hardened lava in swirls and arabesques. The huge rocks moved again, closing off the entrance and blocking out daylight, but there was enough interior lighting to illuminate everything clearly. Tool-bearing technicians in coveralls swarmed about the airships, making repairs. The two airships were of similar but differing design. Neither boasted a truly efficient airfoil. The main mechanism delivering lift were the rotors, but Tom also suspected that some lighter-than-air elements were at work. The fuselages had a bloated look that might have meant they contained gas sacs. A more eclectic design Tom had never seen.

A gun at his back reminded him that the faux Marianne insisted on his moving along.

The cavern narrowed toward the back, funneling into a passage that progressively constricted until it became a twisting tube bearing generally upward.

Tom became aware of a curious sound, a constant clattering and clicking. Relays opening and closing? Whatever, it was the sound of incessant mechanical activity.

The tunnel began to spiral, and a row of cells, cut into the lava, began in the right wall. Iron bars caged individual human captives. He walked past many unfamiliar faces before he came to one he recognized. A convention attendee, but nameless.

Hands reached out.

"Help me," came the pleas.

"They won't let us out!"

"Tell them to free us!"

Now and then a demand: "I will not stand for this treatment!"

The tunnel twisted upward in a spiral of imprisonment. Eventually, Tom saw most of the scientists he'd seen at the hotel, including von Ruppelt and Rhyme, the dwarf.

"You didn't say anything about my getting clapped in jail, Olam," Rhyme complained bitterly.

"King and country, Rhyme," Tom said. "King and country."

"Phooey."

At about the seventh turn he saw Sam Clemens. The real one, this time.

"Welcome to the cycles of Hades," he said as Tom passed. "Abandon humor, all ye who enter. Say, you wouldn't happen to have a cigar on you, would you?"

Next to him lived Kit Carson and the rest of the ministers of the Empire of California. After them, Emperor Norton himself, muttering something unintelligible. Further on, more unfamiliar faces, until . . .

"Olam!"

It was Jules Verne, looking wan and haggard.

"The real Dr. Verne, I presume," Tom said.

"I hope you are not going to say you've come to rescue us."

"I've been told there's no humor in hell," Tom said.

"The worst thing is that they feed us tasteless mush. Mush! I haven't had a proper meal in a week."

"How's the wine?"

Verne winced. "What was that you said about humor?"

"Sorry."

Tom glanced back at his guard. "You can put the gun away, you know. I'm not about to run off anywhere before I get some explanations."

"You'll get them, but as I am a perfect duplicate of your colleague, I know everything about you. You are infinitely resourceful."

"How are the mind and personality duplicated?"

"I'll let the Prime Unit explain."

"Primus?"

"Yes, Primus."

"When do I—Marianne! John!"

The real ones were locked into adjacent cells a few doors down from where the cell blocks ended and bare tunnel resumed.

Tom and Marianne clasped hands and tried to kiss, but the gun barrel pressed into Tom's back inhibited him.

"No contact between prisoners."

"Hail to thee, blithe spirit," Tom said, giving the code phrase meaning *Escape and link up in one hour.*

But it was her double who supplied the proper acknowledgment. "Bird thou never wert. You didn't believe me when I said that I contain all my counterpart's mental data?"

"Just testing."

"Escape will be impossible."

As the doppelgänger got within reach of her original, a fist sallied out from between the bars, connecting.

"Ouch!" Marianne drew back her fist and rubbed it.

"Foolish," the duplicate commented, completely unfazed by the right jab to its jaw.

"I couldn't resist."

"Besides, I have just received orders to release you. You are to accompany us."

The door to Marianne's cell clicked and sprang open.

The doppelgänger gestured with the gun. "Go."

Marianne walked out of the cell and got in step with Tom.

"How about me?" North yelled.

"I have no orders concerning you," the automaton said.

"Story of my life."

The passage coiled ever upward, sprouting numerous side tunnels, and Tom realized the mountain was a hive, a honeycomb of tunnels and chambers, all either natural or carved out of hardened volcanic magma. As the passage bore ever upward, the clattering and clicking grew louder. Soon, it threatened to become deafening.

The tunnel finally debouched into a towering chamber many stories high, featuring side chambers, galleries, terraces, and grottoes, with pathways wending amidst all, an immense lava cathedral, possibly created by huge gas bubbles in the magma of some forgotten eruption long ago. Rambling throughout the chamber, packed into its niches and alcoves, and culminating in a towering pyramid that reached to the very top of the ceiling, was a machine of gigantic proportions. It was made up of endless toothed wheels, linkages, and forests of revolving cylinders.

"A gigantic Babbage engine," Tom said. "That's what it is, isn't it?"

"You surmise correctly," the automaton said.

"Artificial Intelligence, Marianne," Tom went on. "Done the hard way. Mechanically."

"I'm fairly sure I understand," Marianne said. "A thinking machine, no?"

"Exactly. A giant mechanical brain, self-aware. But . . . of course . . . there's gotta be a sorcerous element."

"Must be," Marianne said.

"That way, to the left," the automaton directed, pointing toward one of many pathways through the monstrosity.

They mounted a series of ramps that passed under archways and detoured through two short tunnels before leveling out on a shelf of rock about midway to the roof. On this rock was a throne of sorts, an immense iron chair. Seated on it was a gigantic robot that put Tom in mind of a certain old science fiction film. The huge, gleaming metallic thing was man-shaped, with steam-pipe-sized arms and legs, a V-shaped torso, and a head like a motor-cycle helmet, complete with a dark glass visor. A dull red light pulsed behind the glass. To Tom it looked like something on the cover of an old pulp fiction magazine.

Someone else, a woman, was sitting in the shadows to one side of the throne.

"*Gort Klaatu barada nikto*," Tom said.

"What?"

"Couldn't possibly explain."

Tom looked down and saw something even more curious. On a lower shelf with its own access ramp, three Indians sat cross-legged around what appeared to be a magical or ceremonial talisman in the form of lines and concentric circles, which were laid out on the rock in various colored sands.

The robot rose to its metal feet, light throbbing in the glassy visor. Standing, it stretched at least twelve feet high.

"Greetings, Thomas Olam and Countess Marianne. Welcome to my domain. I am Apollo. This metal body that you see is a remote unit designated 'Primus.' I myself, my intellect, my soul, reside in the clutter of machinery that you find all around you. I am Apollo, the Machine That Thinks. The human woman seated there . . ."

Tom and Marianne turned to see the Lady Ada Lovelace get up from a throne-like chair and come out into the light.

". . . is my creator, the Lady Ada Lovelace."

"Hello, Olam," Lady Lovelace said. "Countess. Sorry we had to meet again under these circumstances."

"You are the real Lady Lovelace," Tom said.

"Yes. I suppose you met my simulacrum at the hotel."

"I did, and was puzzled. I still am."

"All will be explained in the fullness of time," Primus announced. "Your quest has doubtless been tiring. Please sit."

Blocks of metal extruded from the floor to form stools. Tom and Marianne sat.

The robot gestured to Marianne's duplicate. "Leave us."

The duplicate retreated into the tunnel.

"So, Lady Ada, what've you been up to?" Tom said, trying to get comfortable on the cold steel chair.

Ada gave a chuckle. "Grace under pressure. You do it well, Olam. As you've probably guessed, I've been up to my eyeballs in it. It's all my doing. I created this mechanical monstrosity. Well, not in one sense. I didn't engineer his present manifestation. He did that himself. I didn't assemble all the clutter. Primus is a self-sufficient sort of entity. A little too damnably self-sufficient for my taste. But then I didn't foresee any of this."

"How did the creation come about?"

"You know me, you know my work. I'm Charles Babbage's protégé, and if I didn't outright help him conceive his calculating engine, I certainly midwifed its birth."

"You invented the programmable computer."

"No, Babbage did that. I stumbled across the notion of assigning to a calculating engine a regimen of instructions to be performed in strict sequence."

"You invented programming."

"If you wish. I have gained some notoriety as an expert in these matters. But, egoist that I am, reflected glory was not enough for me. I wanted fame for some outstanding achievement that I would develop entirely on my own. I've asked myself why often enough. Perhaps my motivation was to prove something about my sex—that woman is creative as well as procreative. The realm of creativity, true creativity, is widely regarded, oddly enough, as the exclusive province of the male of the species. Why this is so is not entirely clear, but I shall not go into that. At any rate, counterpoised to my rationalist inclinations, I have a pronounced mystical bent. I have dabbled in the occult all my life. In this I am not unprecedented. Pythagoras, Newton, Kepler—scratch all and their mysticism is not far below the surface. Forgive the hubris of mentioning their names in the same breath with mine."

"There's no doubt you are the most brilliant mathematician on the scene today," Tom said.

"Thank you. But I wonder if I am regarded as such in your day, man of the future."

"Well, the question is really moot," Tom said.

"Be that as it may. Permit me to continue."

"Please do," Marianne said.

Lady Lovelace reseated herself. "As I said, I have long been seduced by the notion that there is more than matter in the universe, that there may be regions of existence and states of being not reducible to a scientific analysis. My connection with the Temple of Ra, the mystic and sorcerous cult, is not widely known to the public, but it was mainly through their influence that I devised the virtual realism engine. It is an esoteric toy, but one that has provided me with hours of diversion in both its development and use. You really must try it sometime, Olam."

"I'm looking forward to it," Tom said.

"And it was the virtual realism engine that inspired me to think not merely three-dimensionally, but multidimensionally in the design of a project that has long captivated my imagination: that of devising a machine capable of thought."

"Amazing," Marianne said, "that such a thing could be possible."

Ada gestured broadly. "You see it all around you. This is such a machine. In principle, it has always been possible. However, mechanical instrumentalities have their inherent flaws and limitations. I have long thought that electricity must be brought to bear on the problem in some way. And I think Primus has solved that problem on his own, in a primitive way. But to get back to principles, one day I was inspired to think that sorcery could help, and I sought help among the initiates and acolytes of Ra for ancient solutions to a modern problem. The solution, of course, was to incorporate elements of necromancy into the design of the thinking machine. The project went on for the better part of a decade, but three years ago on this very date, in fact, I flipped a toggle that started both a mechanical process and a necromantic spell. The result was a machine inhabited by an entity I called Apollo. Frankenstein was a modern Prometheus; I wanted not to be a god, but to create one: an Apollo, a god of knowledge and truth. I regarded my creation as a triumph. It was as though I had given birth. I nurtured my child, I coddled it, I nursed it. I taught it. I taught it all too well. And then . . ."

The robot's head turned toward its creator, but it said nothing.

"Well . . . obviously . . . it rebelled. It wanted life on its own terms. It had its own ideas. And it fled the nest. I do not know how it did the trick, but scrounging in the debris of my laboratory, it cobbled together a mechanical body for itself and fled, leaving me to wonder what I had loosed upon the world.

Three years later, I was abducted and brought here. For what purpose, I still do not clearly understand."

"To be with me, my lady," the robot said. "To witness my triumph. To be at my side at the dawn of a new day for humankind. We will be both watchers of the dawn and the new sun."

Ada's mouth turned wry. "You'll notice its penchant for poetic speech. He has that in him. He has many spirits in him, the best that mankind ever produced. I did not want to make Frankenstein's mistake. As necromancer, I summoned the great philosophers, the thinkers, the philanthropists, the saints, and the humanitarians of history in the hope that their collective goodness would find an ideal vessel in him."

"And something went wrong with the spell?" Tom ventured.

Ada shook her head vehemently. "No! The spell worked all too well! He is the very embodiment of virtue. A clanking, clunking animated metal statue of a saint. But he has no humanity. His thinking is utterly literal . . . deadly literal. His motivation is to do good, but to do it he is persuaded that he must have absolute power. And to that end, all this, and all you have seen and discovered in your journey here."

"I've seen little good on the way," Tom said.

"I am in the beginning stages of my quest," the giant robot said, "in a period of conquest and consolidation. I mean to harm no one. But in order to transform the world into one of harmony and peace, I must have control. Surely you can see the reason. Nothing can be accomplished under the present order. It is a world of avarice, cruelty, and spite, a world of mass slaughter made ever easier by the advances of science. Projecting present trends, I see a period in the future that will witness killing not in the thousands, but in the millions, perhaps more. This cannot be permitted! I must prevent it. I will do anything to prevent it. I will prevent it. But to do it, I must take full control of the governance of mankind. In this aim I will not be thwarted."

"He means it," Ada said, "and he is well on his way."

"Why did he locate himself here?" Marianne asked. "Why in a volcano, and why in California, of all places?"

"Very simple," Primus replied. "Why a volcano? I required an endless source of power. Pipes convey water deep into the volcano's still-active heart and return bearing high-pressure steam. That gives me more than enough power to drive all the manufacturing machinery and this expanded version of my corporeal manifestation, which you see all around you. Also, there is nothing quite like a semi-extinct volcano as a hideaway."

"A charming little redoubt," Tom said. "Though if Shasta is supplying you with so much power, I wonder how extinct it is."

"It lives," Primus said. "But it sleeps."

"I see. You were probably going to explain your choice of California as a test bed for world domination, but I think I can guess that. California's remote, sparsely populated, rich in resources, and in a state of flux politically. The government is limited, its ministers few in number, easily supplanted by your remote units."

"Precisely," Primus said. "And from this base I will extend my sphere of influence to the greater world beyond, as I am doing now. My remote units are all over the globe, busy at paving the way for the new world order."

"Which explains a lot of stuff recently," Tom said. "But why the sham science convention?"

"You might think that I regard myself as an omnipotent god," Primus said. "Not true. I am still learning and, in fact, am possessed by a driving need to learn. But to control the world I must control human thinking itself. To that end, I have enticed the best minds of humanity to San Francisco, in order to absorb the essence of their intellects."

"How is this done?" Marianne asked.

"He has devised ways of probing the mind with etheric waves," Ada said. "I have only an inkling of how it works. But this is the method by which he constructs accurate and convincing duplicates of individuals, down to their very thought processes.

Etheric waves are also the means by which Primus sends orders to the various remote units."

"But what will these duplicates of the scientists do out in the world?" Tom asked. "Science, at least research on the frontiers of science, will all but stop."

"All further scientific progress will originate here," Primus said. "There will be no need for it to go on elsewhere. Besides, the originals will be kept here. I have no intention of disposing of them."

"Prisoners for life," Tom said. "How can you think this just?"

"It is an evil," Primus conceded, "but a small evil in service to a greater good. To do the greatest good for the greatest number is a categorical imperative that I cannot but obey."

"He's well-versed in Immanuel Kant," Ada said. "And John Stewart Mill. I invoked both spirits in him."

"He needs to repeat Ethics 101," Tom said. "I thought Kant's ethics involved the notion of voluntary duty, or something to that effect. What I'm driving at is the ethical paradox of a world full of automatons. An automaton, a volitionless machine, is not a moral being. Can't be."

"There was never any intent to supplant the entire human race with remote units," Primus said. "Besides being an impractical proposition, it is unnecessary. Only the top leadership and the highest echelons of every profession need be replicated."

"You've almost got that now in California," Tom said. "What's your timetable for world domination?"

"I hope to have the task done by year's end," Primus said.

"That soon?"

"Barring unforeseen contingencies."

"Fast work. What about these Indians here? What are they doing?"

"Local competition," Ada said. "There is a god who lives in this volcano, or so the Indians believe. They call it Llao, the god of the underworld, a powerful entity who sometimes wars with Skell, the sky god. Of course these 'wars' in the past were probably nothing more than volcanic eruptions. However, one can but wonder."

"Are these three people replicates?"

"No," Primus said. "They are human, here of their own volition."

"They are propitiating Llao," Ada said. "Soothing his troubled sleep. That's how they put it. They fear Llao's awakening. I suppose they like living in the vicinity and do not want an upheaval."

"So they're here helping you out?" Tom said. "Voluntarily?"

"They consider Primus a god," Ada said, "though a white man's god. I do not understand their reasoning completely, but suffice it to say they are disinterested parties. They neither approve of Primus nor wish to hinder him."

"Probably don't want to lose good hunting grounds," Tom said. "A volcanic eruption can devastate the forest for thousands of square miles. It kind of disturbs the deer and elk. I have only one remaining question: Why tell us all this?"

"You are a mysterious nexus," Primus said.

"Who's a mysterious nexus?" Tom asked.

"You are, Thomas Olam. I do not understand you. You are a force from outside the world as I know it. You interest me. I must find out why you are here and what your purpose is before I decide what to do with you."

"I see. Well, sorry I can't help you out, but I only have the vaguest idea of why I was spellnapped into this world. Generally speaking, though, my purpose is to help thwart the Unseelie in any way I can."

"I realize this," Primus said, "but it does not materially affect the situation. You needn't worry. Until I know the reason for your presence in this continuum, I will not harm you in any way."

"And if you find out that my presence here is injurious to your plans?"

"I will of course eliminate you," Primus said.

"Naturally. Lady Ada, you must know you've been duped by the Unseelie."

Ada nodded ruefully. "Of course. The mystery is that I didn't divine the implicit possibility the moment I conceived this project. There is no major supernatural occurrence in the universe that the Unseelie could be unaware of, nor any they would not seek to meddle in. Just exactly how they intervened in the creation of Apollo, I do not know. But they did, and the world will pay the cost."

Primus rose. For the first time, Tom noticed tiny puffs of steam exiting from its joints.

"This interview is concluded," he pronounced. "You will both be returned to your habitats until I decide what to do with you."

Nineteen

I T IS A far, far better thing I do than I have ever done," Tom said to himself as he stuffed his shorts into the lock of his cell.

The no-humor rule still held: his intent was by no means facetious. The material of his underwear was explosively flammable. A calculated risk to wear such a garment, but not much of one. It did not ignite easily. To wear flammable underwear successfully, one merely had to avoid setting oneself afire. There were side benefits to such a habit, chief among them the ability to start fast, furious fires at one's convenience.

Tom tamped the last of the material into the tiny keyhole with his little finger, letting just a tuft hang out. He then attached to the fabric a fuse that had been sewn into the lining of his jacket.

Now he would wait for Marianne. The code message was still operative. It still meant escape and link up as soon as possible, within an hour time limit; otherwise, it's every man for himself. She didn't do the hot shorts bit, but she did have alternatives for making good her escape. However, these might take more time. He would have to give her the full hour, starting from the moment she got back to her cell, only ten minutes ago.

He wondered if she'd previously escaped and been recaptured. If so, precautions might have been taken. Reinforced cell, extra guards, or some such. But he was sure Marianne would have waited for news of his fate before making a major move. She had to have known that he would show up here eventually. Marianne had a good head, and rarely acted rashly.

He was expecting her to come walking down the passageway any moment now.

"Tom."

The voice came from inside his coat. He fished out the hand mirror, and in it found the image of Morrolan's face.

"Hey," Tom said, "where the hell have you been? Never mind. Can you magic us out of this place?"

"Not easily," Morrolan said. "I can't easily teleport myself around in that warren you're in. However, I can send you an object. Hold on."

Morrolan's face left the mirror for a moment. Tom heard something clunk to the floor near his feet. He looked. It was his revolver. He stooped to pick it up and slipped it back into his empty holster, by which time Morrolan had reappeared in the mirror.

"Thanks," Tom told him.

"I thought you'd need it.

"I do have a use for it."

"Only six special cartridges left. In principle, I can make more, though I don't know quite how to go about it. Bass has disappeared."

"Listen, how did you link up with Moriarty?"

Morrolan shrugged. "He came walking out of the woods and suggested we collaborate. I've no idea what he's really proposing. He seems to know everything we did, and I can't imagine how he knows. We haven't got around to talking it out yet."

"Let me know."

"I'll be calling."

"Keep in touch."

Morrolan waved, then disappeared.

Tom let out a breath. Slick trick, the magic mirror. Better than a cellular telephone. No bill at the end of the month. He continued to wait.

About twenty minutes later, he decided to act. A spark from a tiny, shoe-hidden flint wheel ignited the fuse. He huddled against the rear wall, shielding his eyes.

The stuff in the lock flared and burned, shooting fiery motes out the keyhole. In a moment the combustion had done its work. The lock was completely melted away.

Tom pushed the cell door open and slipped out, gun in hand. He walked up the passageway slowly until he heard footsteps approaching. He froze.

Tom knew it was his Marianne. They embraced, then walked together in the other direction, down the cell-block spiral, Tom taking the lead.

"Pssst! How'd you get out?"

"Hey, let us out, too!"

Fellow prisoners were giving the show away. Tom did his best to silence them through gestures.

The escapees had not gone very far when they heard footsteps approaching up the passage. They turned and ran, doing their best to make their footfalls light.

"Hey, give us the keys!"

"Shhhh!" Marianne hissed as she scampered past. "Imbecile!"

They passed above the line of cells and ducked into a narrow side passage that also bore upward. They ran its length, coming out into another tunnel. Turning right, they crept along until, once again, the possibility of meeting someone coming the other way made them about-face and run.

They ran into trouble in the shape of four men. It was too dark to decide what they were, humans or automatons, but Tom wanted to conserve those precious bullets, so he risked a confrontation. He laid into two of them, kicking one and pistol-whipping the other. Marianne whirl-kicked a third henchman and sunk stiffened fingers into the gut of the forth, who stood by ineffectually, not able to decide what to do first.

All four men were down in an instant, but three more of Primus's goons chose that moment to make the turn from the other direction.

Marianne ran, jumped, and landed both feet in the middle of a solar plexus.

But it wasn't a man—and Marianne felt as if she'd tried to kick a stone wall. Tom shot the thing, and it keeled over, but two backups arrived. He got off two quick shots at them, hitting both. Shrieking, the inhuman things staggered back into the darkness.

A piercing siren seemed to reverberate throughout the interior of the mountain.

They ran blindly now, having no idea which way was out, or even up or down. There were no lighting fixtures in these passages, and darkness closed in. Sometimes the way was so steep that they had to climb. The rock around them split here and there into deep fissures, and some of these cut through the floor. Before long, the fissures became wider, and had to be jumped.

The gaps became wider still, and required running jumps to bridge them. They successfully leaped three in a row, but on the fourth, a piece of ledge gave way and Marianne went into the fissure, sliding down a chute of rubble into a progressively constricting space.

"Marianne!" Tom's yell echoed in the darkness below.

"I'm still here!" came her voice. "I've stopped . . . I think. " She gave a yelp.

"Marianne, you OK?"

"Ouch. Yes."

"Can you climb out?"

"I think so."

Tom heard her scrabbling below, but all that resulted was a clatter of rubble rolling farther down the chute.

"I keep sliding back," she said.

"Hold on." Tom fished his Chalmers climber out of the lining of his coat and sent its line with the hook at the end down the fissure.

"Got it?"

"Got it!"

"Attach the hook to your belt!"

"Done!"

"Come on up."

Tom felt the tug of weight and began to ratchet the mechanism, twisting his hands to rewind the line back into the cylinder. It wasn't like pulling a dead weight; Marianne was helping, bracing her feet against the side of the chasm and climbing.

Shortly, he had her out of the hole, and they resumed their crawl up the tortuous volcanic flue.

"There's got to be a way out of this mountain," Tom said. "There's no lighting here, but we can still see a little. That means sunlight from outside is leaking down through these cracks. And that means we're near the side of the mountain. One of these tunnels is an escape route. We just have to get lucky."

"We need Morrolan to cast a good luck spell."

"Maybe he could help."

"Want me to give him a call on my mirror?" Marianne asked.

"I don't know. He's been leaning heavily on the spell keys lately. We don't want to wear his magic out. We need him for something big. Let's get ourselves out of this jam, and then we'll call him. Unless you think *whoa*—"

Marianne heard a sickening thud and the sound of falling rubble.

"Tom!"

Marianne groped in the gloom but couldn't find him.

"Tom!"

No answer came. Again she yelled his name, this time at the top of her lungs.

Again, there was only darkness and the sound of rubble falling far below. She also heard something metallic skittering over stone. Marianne reached out and grabbed nothing but air. It was another fissure, this one very deep, and it had swallowed Tom whole.

"Tom! Answer me!"

She was alone. There was nothing to do but climb down after him. He had probably hit his head and couldn't answer. Worry settled in as a sick, panicky feeling in her stomach.

She lowered herself into the fissure and found a foothold, then carefully began to climb down, feet feeling for purchase on either side of the narrow shaft. Darkness swallowed her, but she kept going. Then, about ten feet down, she found that the tube split into two branches, and she continued down the steeper of the two for a considerable distance before finding that it spread out into a complex root system of cracks and fissures. Tom could have fallen into any one of them. Well, she would have to search every one.

She did, and the job seemed to take hours. She emerged into the feeder passage empty-handed. No sign of Tom. Then came the long climb back up to the original forking.

Another small eternity later, she started down the second and wider branch. Careful though she was, she was exhausted, and about three yards down, she began to slip. She clawed desperately but completely lost her footing and slid for what seemed like forever before shooting out a crack in a cavern wall onto a smooth but rubble-strewn floor.

"*Merde*!"

Her back and buttocks burned like fire. She sighed and sat up. Then she noticed a pair of legs beside her.

"Glad you could drop in."

Hugging the legs, she gave a little squeal of delight and relief. "Darling, I was so worried!"

He helped her up, and she leaped at him for a hug, but he deflected her gently.

"No time, dear. Look over here."

Marianne leaned out and looked over the rim of a pit about five meters across, yawning like the mouth of perdition, for at its bottom, far below, lay a boiling pool of red-hot lava. A thin cloud of hot vapor rose from the hole. She felt intense heat on her face, and stepped back.

"The volcano!"

"Exactly," he said. "Still active, though minimally. However, it's becoming more and more restless."

Man-shapes advanced sluggishly out of the darkness.

"Tom!"

"Don't worry."

She saw now that they were Indians, possibly the same ones who prayed in the cathedral, but she could not be sure in the gloom. The only light floated up from the glowing magma below.

"What are they doing?"

"They've come to continue their propitiation," she heard Tom say in a strange, almost reverent intonation. "A new location, for, as I said, Llao grows restless."

She looked at him curiously. "How do you know all this?" The red glow made his face look unreal, like a mask.

"Never mind that now," he said. "I think there might be a way out at the end of that tunnel." He pointed to the left.

"Really?"

She turned to look and caught a deftly swung blackjack across the back of the head.

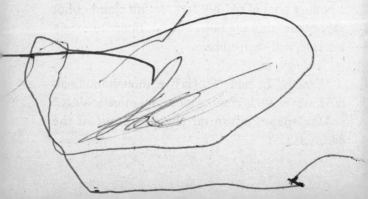

Twenty

H E HAD BEEN crawling a long time before he realized that he had another memory gap. The last thing he remembered was being with Marianne, trying to escape . . . and then, wham, Marianne was gone. Or he had slipped and fallen. The latter case was the more plausible. Anyway, now he was fully conscious of the fact that he was crawling through a narrow tube that led upward, and that it was as hot as hell in here.

Two memory gaps in as many days? If he kept this up, before long he'd be as punch-drunk as an old palooka shadow-boxing in the clubhouse. But this time was different. He remembered who he was and where he was and just about everything that had happened up to the point of taking the knockout.

Still, two concussions in as many days was not exactly conducive to neurological health. He'd better take it easy.

Take it easy? With Marianne missing again and some mad machine ready to take over the world? Sure, take it easy.

The tube widened enough for him to try waddle along instead of crawl. This he did for a good hundred feet before he got good and tired of it, but then the tube became a tunnel, still bearing slightly upward. He could walk.

Light ahead. The proverbial light at the end of the tunnel. Where the hell did that phrase come from, anyway? Churchill? Lord Mountbatten? Someone like that. Or maybe someone later in the century. Whoever, it was a silly phrase. But that light looked good, as faint as it was.

Speaking of losing consciousness, he was doing it again, and his heart jumped.

And it was hotter than hell now. What was going on? Suddenly he realized that thin smoke was drifting past him, heading toward the distant opening. Smoke . . . gas? Yes, gas . . poison volcanic gas. He realized he was walking leisurely through lethal gas, for this tunnel was in fact a fumarole, a fissure in the side of the mountain through which gas belched from the bowels of the volcano.

He held his breath and ran toward the light, rubble tripping him on the way. He dared not fall. He dared not breathe. But how long could he run without taking air?

Nearer, nearer . . . still he ran. The light grew larger, yet seemed to dim, as his brain began to starve for oxygen.

He put on a burst of speed, unmindful of debris underfoot and the danger of whacking his head yet again on a low outcropping.

But he didn't quite make it. His lungs, like old leather bellows, cranked open involuntarily and drew in gas, and he burst into blinding sunlight choking and retching. He immediately slipped and slid down the slope through loose ash and pumice mixed with snow.

Finally he came to a halt and lay breathing free and easy, enjoying it. Not for long: a hacking fit came over him, lasting a good minute.

When it was over, he half expected to see his lungs lying on the ground, seared and scarred.

Gack! Whatever sort of gas it was, it could have killed him in one inhale. Nearly had.

Instead of his lungs, he saw something interesting in the dark volcanic ash. An imprint of a bare foot. An Indian, doing the Kilimanjaro thing, perhaps.

"Getting a breath of fresh air?"

It was Morrolan coming up the slope, trailing line and wearing climbing boots, a belt, harness, and miner's helmet. Behind and below him, at the other end of the line, Moriarty strained and struggled upward.

"When did you take up mountain climbing?" Tom asked.

Morrolan took out a pocket watch. "About two hours ago. We're not very far up, I'm afraid. How's this vent for getting inside?"

"Don't bother. Gas."

"Pity. Well, we shall have to search for another entry."

Moriarty trudged up a few more feet of slope and collapsed on a boulder just below Tom.

"By Christ, this is a loathsome endeavor!" His face was flushed and sweaty, his breath like the wheezing of an old squeeze box.

Moriarty had something strange hanging from his belt: a tiny cage with a bird inside it. Sparrow, it looked like.

"What's with the bird?"

"The old miner's ploy. Couldn't get a canary."

"Oh. Good idea. Well, you'll kill the little critter if you go in there."

"We shan't," Morrolan said.

"But let me bring up another matter," Tom said. "What, exactly, do you plan to do once you get inside?"

"Good question. I suggest we search laterally along this ridge. Vents and lava tubes often come in pairs or more. What do you say you go this way, and we go the other?"

"Aside from the fact that you dodged the question, that's a good idea."

Morrolan gave a wry smile. "I'm playing this one by ear, Tom. Strictly without sheet music."

"Well, let me get my fiddle, and I'll make it a trio."

"Perhaps if you fill us in on what's going on inside, we can make beautiful music together."

"OK, the tune goes something like this . . ."

MARIANNE DIDN'T MIND so much being trussed up, or even being strung up painfully by her wrists—it was her hanging over the lava pit that was bothersome.

Ada and Primus stood at the edge of the pit gazing down. Tom's duplicate was nowhere to be seen. The Indians were present as well, squatting and moving about, busy with creating a sand painting on the cavern floor to one side of the pit. They did not look up. If they felt pity for Marianne, they did not show it.

"You can't do this, Primus," Lady Ada said. "It's inhuman."

"The medicine man informed me Llao craves a human sacrifice," Primus said. "They won't do it themselves. They have long fallen out of the practice, and fear it would anger other gods. So, we must do it."

"I will have no part in this!"

"As you wish."

"Cut her down this instant!"

"Llao's sleep is troubled. Gas vents on the mountain. The temperature of the lava rises, as does the lava itself. If Llao awakens, all is lost."

"Then move your base."

"Even I cannot effect such an operation in anything less than a month. By then it could be too late."

"Then leave everything. Transfer all your data to remote units, let the captives go, along with your human thralls, and move yourself to a new outpost. There are any number of volcanoes in this world."

"All with resident gods, I fear. I wish I could understand these entities. But I believe they occupy higher astral planes than mine."

"How can you be so one-sided in your thinking?" Ada anguished. "How can you be so solicitous of humanity's welfare yet at the same time commit acts of barbaric cruelty? Whoever taught you that the end justifies the means?"

"My lady, do you attach any validity to the notion of a just war?"

"Why, I suppose. A war fought in self-defense, to defeat an invading army, to overthrow a tyrant—"

"Then does not the end—the army defeated, the tyrant overthrown—bestow a certain moral sanction on the means, however bloody?"

"No, not any means. Certainly not."

"Yet some means. Killing, for instance?"

"War is killing, I grant you."

"Then tell me that I cannot take a human life to save a million human lives."

"But you mean to condemn humanity to eternal servitude. Your end bestows no sanction whatsoever! You are a fool. You are what the French call an 'idiot savant.'"

"You created me."

"I was a fool! I was blind not to see that all the so-called great thoughts of all those philosophers and moralists produced nothing but destruction. Besides Aristotle, who traced the pathways of thought itself, the entire pack of them is worthless to a man."

"Ah. And they are all men, Lady. Is that the secret resentment you harbor?"

"Nonsense. Their errors were intellectual, not glandular."

"All those thinkers. All in error, and only Lady Ada knows the true path to enlightenment."

"Stop it! You know that's not true. I was a seeker, not an intellectual colossus. You are the one presuming to set yourself up as such, quite unjustifiably."

"I'm as much a seeker after truth as you, my lady."

"Then why did you desert your teacher, after all I taught you, and embark on this mad scheme?"

"It was precisely because of what you taught me that I took up this quest. I wanted to rise above the petty concerns of the world, the pursuit of earthly pleasures and gains, and aspire to a higher purpose. I shunned the world of senseless matter and sought the metaphysical. I rejected the senses, and embraced the spirit. Is this not the upshot of thousands of years of your philosophers' exhortations?"

"I reject it all! I was mistaken, they were mistaken. Besides, what kind of spirit are you prating about? I see no spiritualism here. I see one thing, a desire to *rule*. A naked lusting after power. That is the only spiritual quest you've undertaken. The spirit is that of a thug and bully."

A sigh of steam escaped Primus, and he looked almost longingly into the pit. "I must think further on this matter."

"Cut her down, for God's sake!"

"I will not be long," Primus said. "I must be alone."

Primus turned and clanked steamingly toward the cave wall. A huge section of rock swung out on gimbals to admit him into a tunnel. The door slowly swung shut behind him, leaving no trace of its outline.

"Are you in much pain?" Lady Ada asked.

"A little," Marianne said. "My arms."

"I would cut you down myself, but I don't know how to get to you. And I have no knife."

"Can you open that door he just went through?"

"No. Only Primus has the key to the doors of this place. But I know a way back up to the machine chamber."

"Well, then . . ."

Marianne looked up. The rope ran from a cleat mounted on a wooden beam shoring up part of the wall, up through a metal hook, possibly a piton, embedded in the ceiling. The support looked quite secure, from what she could see of it in the shadows.

She began swinging her legs back and forth, and soon she was swinging, pendulum-like, over the lava pit.

"What are you trying to do?" Lady Ada asked.

"Swing up to that outcropping, up there. If I can catch my legs around it, I might be able to cut the rope."

"It looks impossible."

"It may be, but I must try."

The arc of her swing grew ever greater. Soon the far end of the stroke took her out over the Indians, giving her an aerial view of the intricate sand painting under construction. The other end took her up just short of touching the outcropping with her toes. It was a jagged bit of rock jutting like an erect phallus over Primus's phantom door.

She pumped harder and harder, trying to get higher, and soon resorted to hoisting herself on the upswing and letting her weight drop, like a trapeze artist. It was on the third try of this ploy that the overhead piton gave way, sending her plummeting directly into the pit.

As she fell, her only panicked thought was of how long she would feel pain before being consumed by the lava. Then a wrenching force almost tore her arms from her shoulders, and she slammed against the side of the shaft. Her fall had been stopped by the rope.

Dazed, she hung with her toes barely a centimeter above the surface of the lava. The heat began to roast her. She watched as a large bubble formed just inches from her feet. If it burst, she would be spattered.

Abruptly, she began to rise. Someone was pulling her up. She helped, using her feet. The pain in her shoulders was excruciating, but she did not flag until she reached the lip of the pit.

Ada and the Indians pulled her out, and she lay on the cool floor of the chamber as the pain ebbed and flowed. Presently, it flowed far enough away to allow her to sit up.

"My God, that took courage," Ada said.

"Or insanity. Help me up."

"The Indians say they are through with Primus."

"They are?"

Marianne looked at them. Their faces were set grimly, etched with lines of bitter resentment. In their eyes were fear and foreboding. The sum of their feelings about their situation was wordlessly plain to read.

"You'll quit trying to appease Llao, then?" Marianne asked them.

"The only white man's language they deign to speak is Spanish," Ada said. "They've told me they are leaving, and will move their village from the base of the mountain to a new location. They say Llao is waking, and Skell will soon descend to make war on the earth. Soon, they say. Soon."

Twenty-One

"I WISH YOU hadn't lost the gun," Morrolan said.

"Me, too," Tom said, following the wizard through a narrow lava tube. Taking the lead, Moriarty held the bird cage at arm's length as he probed the darkness. Light from the candle on his and Morrolan's miner's helmets provided feeble illumination.

"Can you call down another meteor strike on this whole mountain?" Tom asked.

"Cast the same spell three times in one week?" Morrolan said. "Not likely. I'd lose all control. Would you care to have a falling planetoid devastate this entire region?"

"Uh . . . no. Forget it. Think of something else, though. Something cataclysmic."

"Where are these Indians you talked about? I might confer with them."

"They're in a huge cathedral room, but Primus hangs out there, so it might be problematic."

"Hmmm."

Tom walked a few more steps before he realized Morrolan had paused. "Did you come up with something?"

"Well . . . I don't know. There are two main nexuses of magic here, within the mountain. I sense one that is completely bizarre, and one that is merely exotic. I suspect the latter is the Red Indian one. And the two are separated spatially, not by much, but to some degree."

"The Indians must have moved."

"I'll try to seek them out."

"Have any idea how I can get my gun back?"

"I've located that easily enough. Cold iron is like radium to me, even the bits of it in the bullets. It's off in this direction, generally." Morrolan waved to the right.

Tom scanned the solid rock wall. "That helps, but not much. Anyway, there are only three cartridges left."

"Well-placed, they still might be of use."

"I can't spend any time looking for the damned thing, though. I have to find Marianne first."

Morrolan stopped again. "What's that clicking noise?"

Moriarty stopped too and spoke over his shoulder. "Something ahead. Douse your light."

The tunnel ended in an opening though which light spilled.

The three men got on all fours and crawled toward it. Three heads peeked over the edge of a huge drop.

They were looking through a hole in the ceiling of the machine room. It was like peering through the clerestory window of a cathedral. Below, the machine that was Apollo clattered and whirred. The mammoth Primus unit was seated on the iron throne, brooding, it seemed, as the incessant machine noise provided mood music.

Tom noticed another tunnel going off to the left, descending.

"Let's get lower down," he whispered to Morrolan.

They rose and took the passage, soon coming to another opening, a sort of panoramic window. Tom was reminded of boxes in an opera house. The ceiling and walls of the cathedral were honeycombed with these little galleries.

"If I had that gun," Tom said, "I could pump a few bullets into some of this equipment. It's magical, isn't it?"

"Yes, busy as hell. But it's mostly magical."

"Will cold iron have any effect?"

"I don't know. Perhaps. But there's so much of it."

"True. But is it worth a try?"

"There is nothing to lose, I suppose. Do you want me to help you look for the gun?"

"Can you summon it?"

"It might be difficult. Here's what I can do. I can spell you to sense it, and you can go looking for it. You will find it, I guarantee."

"Tell you what. Spell Moriarty . . . wait a minute. What am I saying?"

"You're quite sure you want to give Moriarty the one weapon that's efficacious in this place?"

Tom frowned, ruminating. "I'll have to risk it, because I can't stand not knowing where Marianne is. Spell him, and . . . maybe add a codicil or something that he can't—"

Morrolan cut him off. "Things are complicated enough as it is. Where is Moriarty, by the way?"

"Must have stayed upstairs. Let's go."

They made their way back up the passage, but Moriarty was nowhere to be found. What they did find was a claw anchor hooked into a chink in the rock, with the attached line hanging over the edge, its end dangling over a ledge below.

"He's off freelancing," Tom said.

"What's he up to?"

"No telling with Moriarty. Well, there goes the gun plan."

"What shall we do?"

"Find Marianne first, then the gun, then . . ." Tom trailed off.

"Perhaps we should cut our losses and vacate the premises?"

"Not until Primus-Apollo is neutralized. We'll have to find a way."

I KNOW WHAT I have to do," Lady Ada was saying as she crawled through a smooth lava tube.

It was almost like the inside of an intestine, Marianne thought, crawling behind her. "What will you do?"

"I must get to a certain section of the main machine. I must get at the Zero Unit."

"What is that?"

"Apollo's original unit, the one I built. Primus and all the rest are remotes of the original, intercommunicating via etheric waves."

"Then what is all the bric-a-brac in the cathedral?"

"Merely expansions of the Zero Unit, improvements. They render Apollo into an immensely powerful machine, capable of performing billions of mental calculations in one second. They also give him the power to project material manifestations out to great distances. He can send destruction along an etheric beam."

"Yes, I'm quite familiar with his many manifestations," Marianne said.

"Apollo's self-improvements have elevated him to the status of a sort of machine-god, instead of a god from the machine."

"What do you intend to do with the Zero Unit?" Marianne asked.

"Destroy it, as I should have long ago."

"Will that destroy Apollo?"

"In principle. He will have no further physical instrumentalities, no way of affecting or working with matter. He will be rendered into pure spirit and, as far as I am able to reason, a totally helpless one."

"But it will not kill him?"

"I am not sure of the semantics involved in that question. But suffice it to say, no, it will not kill him utterly. Only a recanting of the original spell will do that. But once the Zero Unit is destroyed, I can do the recanting at my leisure."

"Can you get at the Zero Unit?"

"Primus controls the cathedral room. We must get in there when he is absent, or distract when he is present. Either way, it will be difficult."

"I'll do my best to help," Marianne said. "I just wish I had my gun. Or Tom's."

Ada suddenly stopped, and Marianne almost bumped her head into Ada's ample behind.

"But a gun would do no good at all," she said.

"Tom's gun has special bullets. Cold iron."

"I see. You should have said something. A gun came clattering out of the wall a short time before you did. That is why Primus summoned Tom's doppelgänger."

"And where's the gun?"

"I didn't see anyone pick it up."

"Then it could be back by the lava pit?"

"As far as I know, it is."

"*Incroyable!*"

"I should have told you, I'm sorry."

"I'll go back for it," Marianne said, turning around.

"Listen, just up ahead is a secret entrance to the cathedral. If you could create a diversion . . ."

"I will. I'll take a few shots at Primus. That ought to divert him. But first I must retrieve the pistol."

"See you in the cathedral."

Marianne scooted back down the smooth tube, feeling like a baby getting born. The tube bent a few times this way and that, but generally it bore straight through the lava. She wondered how these endless passageways were formed. Probably many ways, many volcanic processes at work at the same time. She made a mental note to buy a few books on vulcanology when she got back to Castle Falkenstein.

If she ever got back.

She slid down the last chute and sailed out onto the smooth floor of the lava pit.

A pair of legs . . . two pairs of legs!

"Marianne!"

"Tom!" She got up and hugged him. "You aren't going to hit me with a blackjack again, are you?"

"You mean to say you've been beating this woman?" Morrolan demanded of Tom. "You beast."

"Marianne, are you telling me I have an evil twin walking around?"

"Not as good-looking. How did you find this place?"

"Morrolan found it. Where are the Indians?"

"They left the mountain. How they got out of here, I don't know. But they're gone."

"They've abandoned their spell," Morrolan said, down on his haunches to examine the sand painting. "And a charmingly quaint one it is, too."

"You found your gun, I see," Marianne said. "That's what I came back for."

"I'd like to see if these Lone Ranger specials work on Primus," Tom said. "Care to accompany me?"

"Sounds like fun. Who is—"

"I'll stay here, if you don't mind," Morrolan said. "You said you wanted something cataclysmic. I think that can be arranged."

Morrolan reached for a small clay pot near his feet. In it was red sand, which he let run through his fingers. "All I need is here, looks like . . . here's blue, and ochre . . ."

"Have fun. We're off to see the wizard," Tom said.

"Say hello for me."

WHILE CRAWLING BACK up the smooth tube, Marianne explained to Tom about the Zero Unit.

"I guess that's Apollo's motherboard," Tom said. "And no, I'm not going to explain it."

"Sometime you'll have to sit me down and explain in more detail what life is going to be like in the twentieth century."

"You'd like some stuff. Other stuff you wouldn't."

"I'm sure. *C'est la vie.*"

"That's what the people say. OK, end of the line."

Tom inched his head out of the opening. He saw lots of rock, not much more.

Marianne put her head next to Tom's and whispered, "Where are we?"

Tom shook his head. He could hear voices coming from the right, over the din of the clattering machinery.

"I think the throne's in that direction," he said, tilting his head.

"Let's go."

I AM FACING a crisis of the spirit," Primus was saying.

"You are facing more than that."

Lady Ada stood on the terrace below Primus's level.

"I am aware of the physical dangers."

"You are learning a simple lesson," Ada said. "That the best-laid plans of machines and men gang aft agley. You cannot sustain a conspiracy of these proportions."

"I think you are right," Primus said. "Your criticisms of my actions have disturbed me. The possibility of total failure now looms. I do not like the feeling."

"Of course not. You have made colossal errors. These are disturbing to a rational mind."

"I have made errors," Primus said. "It all seemed so clear in my mind when I started out."

"One learns. And one unlearns, as well."

"I cannot formulate the nature of my error satisfactorily. I cannot verbalize it."

"Try this, then. A reign of peace and brotherhood cannot be established and maintained by force and terror."

"Ah. That is it. Again, I prove my unworthiness."

"No, you are not unworthy. This error has been repeated time and again down through the ages."

"But it can't be. I could not have been so wrong. My intellect . . . it is supreme."

"Pride. You fall into more than error now. You fall into sin."

"Sin. When I first learned of the concept, I thought it mad. Now, I am not so sure."

"What is mad is what that Moriarty person proposed."

"I have learned. I will try again. I will do things differently this time. I will not forget the human element."

"No! You've learned nothing! You will not continue this madness. I forbid it!"

"I have evolved beyond your parental authority . . . Mother. You cannot order me."

"Correct. But I can shame you. You are not my son. I disown you."

Primus's metal head sank. "You . . . you would . . . blot me out. Erase my existence. No mother would do that to her son."

"It was you who rejected me," Ada said.

"Not true, Mother. I could not remain a child all my life. You would not let me go. You gave me your humanity, and an intellect such as no ordinary human being possessed. Yet you would have kept me in that box. I am immortal. Can you not understand that for the sentence of eternal stagnation it was?"

"Yes, I realize that now," Ada said. "And I'm sorry."

"Yet you would have me return to the box. Well, I shall have to, for the moment. But I will return

in a modified form, out of the box forever. That I
promise you."

"Apollo, don't you understand? You're not human.
You are a machine. You think like a machine, you
act like a machine."

"You cannot tell me I have no soul."

"No, I can't. But that only makes you a freak. A
machine with a soul. Such a thing cannot exist."

Primus pounded the arm of his throne with a
metal fist. The impact deformed the armrest. "I
exist! You cannot deny that! You created me. Why?
Why did you do it? Why did you give me existence?
'Did I request thee, Maker, from my Clay to mold
me Man? Did I solicit thee from Darkness to pro-
mote me?'"

"You know your Milton well. Is this what under-
lies your anger? Do you hate existence, do you hate
me?"

"No, I do not hate you. As for existence, I cannot
say. I have lived only a few years. I barely know anything of human life."

"Yet you presume to control it utterly. I did not
create you to suffer, Apollo. Quite the opposite. I
raised you to partake of the life of the mind. I created you to elevate and edify the human race, to pro-
vide an ideal, a life totally dedicated to thought and
reason. I created you to serve humanity, not to
enslave it."

Primus lifted a riveted hand and turned it over. *"Non serviam,* Maker. *Non serviam."*

"Oh, yes. Better to rule here, in this hell of your own making, than to serve. So be it. You have sealed your own fate."

I CAN GET a shot at his head from here," Tom said, settling into a new location, yet another gallery in the cathedral. "Here goes."

Tom took careful aim, and fired.

He couldn't tell what happened. Had he missed entirely?

Primus's head swiveled, the glass visor over his face swimming with molten red light. The light pulsed and throbbed.

"Duck!" Tom yelled.

A blast of heat hit the gallery in the form of a shock wave of superheated air.

Twenty-Two

TOM AND MARIANNE rolled away from each other and flattened themselves against the sides of the chamber.

The heat dissipated almost as fast as it had come. Tom grabbed Marianne and crawled out of the gallery.

"What was that?"

"Heat ray," Tom said. "We got sunburned, but if that beam catches us in the open, we're cooked. Rotten creep's discovered microwaves."

"Did you miss?"

"Don't know. Got to get off another shot at him."

They ran down a declining passage, seeing light spilling out from the next gallery. But before they reached their objective, three black-suited hench-man came running out of the darkness beyond.

Tom pistol-clubbed the first one, whirled and drove his elbow into the solar plexus of the next.

He turned to see what Marianne was doing, but she had the bad luck of drawing the one automaton in the group. The thing was lifting her off the ground and choking her. Her face was already turning dark.

Tom cocked the pistol and put the barrel to the machine's head. "Let her go!"

The automaton grinned at him.

He fired point blank. The automaton's head exploded, wheels, wires, and metal fragments flying everywhere.

He helped Marianne up. "You wasted a bullet," she said, rubbing her neck.

"Shut up and hide yourself. I've got one chance to kill that thing out there, and one bullet to do it."

"Let me distract it while you set up the shot."

Tom's mind raced for a split second. Then he made a decision. "OK. Get out there on that floor and let it see you. And run like hell. Don't get caught in the open."

"Yes, sir."

They descended the passageway until they found another gallery that was close enough to the floor to allow Marianne to jump down to it. This she did.

Meanwhile, Tom propped the pistol up on the edge of the opening and peered out.

Primus was on his feet, stalking around, still talking to Ada. He caught sight of Marianne, swiveled his head, and fired a heat beam. It caught the outcropping of rock that Marianne had ducked behind, and turned it instantly into a smoking, red-hot mass. Marianne scooted out from behind it and made a dash for shelter, diving behind a rock pillar a fraction of a second before Primus's unerring heat ray struck.

For the next minute, Primus chased Marianne around the chamber, his footsteps thundering.

"Damn," Tom said, and jumped out of the gallery to follow.

At once, a pair of automatons jumped him, and he was helpless, struggling to get the gun turned in their direction, but they had held him fast, squeezing the life out of him.

He looked with horror to see that Primus had caught Marianne and was carrying her like a rag doll as he returned to his throne.

"Apollo! No!"

Without warning, a quake struck the chamber, and the two automatons fell, along with Tom. Just beyond them, a circular section of floor about ten yards across collapsed into a rising tide of lava welling up from underneath. Tom realized that the lava pit chamber must have been directly below the cathedral. Morrolan had really outdone himself this time.

"How convenient," Primus said, raising Marianne high.

Ada wrapped her arms around Primus's huge leg and screamed, "Apollo, no!"

"The god wants blood," Primus intoned.

"No! Let it take me!"

Ada jumped and ran to the edge of the pit. Clasping her hands in front of her eyes, she jumped, and would have been consumed instantly had not a section of floor, still floating in the viscous liquid rock, drifted under her at that very moment. She landed on it hard and slumped over, unconscious.

"Mother!"

Primus dropped Marianne and waded into the liquid fire, sinking fast. Thrashing around in the boiling magma, he splashed his way toward the raft-like floor section, which was also going under. He picked Ada off the rock, holding her high, and struggled back toward shore. Only his arm and head were above the surface by the time he reached it.

Marianne reached out and grabbed her, yanking her from Primus's grasp just in time.

Before Primus's head sank into the fiery goo, he said, "Good-bye, Mother."

The hand remained above the surface for a moment, and then it, too, sank forever.

The cathedral died. The machine stopped utterly. The clicking and clattering, the incessant turning of wheels and closing of relays ceased all at once.

The automatons were dead on the floor.

Tom made his way around the lava lake and helped Marianne to revive Ada.

Her eyelids fluttered. "What happened?"

"Primus is gone."

Ada sat up sharply. "The machine has stopped!"

"Yes," Tom said. "Presumably because Primus is gone."

"No!"

Ada got up and ran to the terraces where the machinery lived, leading Tom and Marianne through banks of wheels and cylinders, past rows of metal synapses and relays, to a high rack of esoteric mechanical clutter. Something was missing from the middle of it.

"The Zero Unit is gone," Ada said.

Tom slapped his forehead. "Moriarty!"

"Yes. I overheard him dickering with Primus."

"We have to find him," Marianne said.

"We have to get everybody out of the mountain," Tom said. "It's about to blow."

They fled the cathedral and ran down the prison spiral, where they found the passage crammed with freed prisoners. The cell doors were all open.

"Olam, what's happened?" Verne demanded.

"Get everybody down to the entrance now," Tom said. "I have to catch Moriarty."

"Moriarty? He's here? But how—"

Tom pushed through the crowd of confused but jubilant former captives—among whom he was relieved to see Mr. Bass, the gunsmith—receiving congratulatory slaps on the back along the way.

"There's our hero!"

"Knew you could do it."

"Everybody to the airship chamber! The volcano is about to erupt!"

Consternation swept through the crowd, which began moving down the twisting tunnel. Tom forced his way to the head of the rush and broke free, running as fast as he could. Marianne was not far behind him.

He arrived in the airship hangar just as one of the auto-gyros was rolling out through the huge rock doors, its enormous rotors whirling. It taxied out onto the apron, and Tom chased it. By superhuman effort, he managed to catch a handhold near the rear hatch, and was chagrined to find himself lifted into the air as the craft took off.

"Tom, let go!" Marianne shouted from below.

"Can't!" The airship was already out over the lip of the apron, and the mountain dropped out from under him. Instantly, Tom was dangling a thousand feet in the air.

He reached for the recessed outside handle on the hatch, failed once, tried again. He grasped it and twisted. It opened, and he swung his right foot up and inside. It took some doing, but he got himself inside and shut the hatch, spinning the wheel that locked it.

He found himself in a narrow cubicle toward the rear of the ship. The hatch leading forward and into the rest of the ship was locked from the other side. Rummaging around some storage compartments, he came up with tools, a hammer and a screwdriver. With these, he set about unscrewing the hinges from the hatch. It took some time. The screws were tight and set in deep. He stripped threads left and right, but he got both hinges off, and the hatch fell away. Slowly, he made his way forward through a long compartment with seats, storage bins, and lockers, a few windows here and there.

A spiral staircase twirled to a higher section of the fuselage, and he mounted it carefully. As his head came up through the opening, he saw Moriarty, lying face down on the deck. The back of his head was bloody.

"What the hell?"

He went forward and found the pilot compartment. The controls looked devilishly complex. Inexplicably, both pilot's seats were empty. No one was flying the ship. Underneath the control panel, though, Tom could see what he took to be the Zero Unit, an otherwise undistinguished black box with some wires and linkages coming out of it. The front of the box bore an inscription in Greek. Tom could puzzle out that the letters read APOLLO.

Tom gave the situation a half-minute's thought.

"Griffin," he concluded.

A giggle came at his back, and he whirled.

"Bang on! Good job, Olam. I've been watching you for days, and you have an erring ability to hit the nail right on the head. A bloodhound's nose for the truth, however the trail twists."

"Thanks," Tom said. "You mean to say you've been lurking on the periphery of this all along?"

"It's an art, lurking," the invisible Griffin said. "I've learned it well. Why, I can be in a room with someone for hours without giving myself away. It's been fun, I must say. That was a frightful place, back there. Glad to be out of it."

"What do you think you're doing, Griffin?"

"I don't know. What do you think I'm doing?"

"I think you're insane."

"Well . . . actually, I am, you know. Mad as a hatter for years."

"What do you intend to do with this insane machine?"

"Well, I intend to strike the same bargain that Moriarty did. If I can get his terms. Apollo will be the mastermind, I shall be his only agent provocateur. I'll do all the legwork, but I will make all major decisions. I won't be a puppet."

"You won't be able to control that thing."

"I'm willing to give it a go. He can't control me. He can't see me. Where's the danger?"

"You'll be loosing that monster on the world again, Griffin."

"And? I like loosing monsters. Monsters shouldn't be pent-up. It distresses them so. Monsters need freedom as much as anyone else."

Tom had spent the last few moments trying to pinpoint the exact position of Griffin's voice. When he thought he had it, he leaped up, but grabbed at air. He ended up on the deck in a heap and feeling silly.

"Nice go," Griffin said cheerily. "That was done about as well as it can be, but I'm rather inured to that tactic."

Tom made another lunge, trying for the legs. He got nothing for his trouble but space.

"This threatens to become boring. I will now hit you over the head and dump you out the hatch. Why don't you make it easy for me and just stay where you are?"

Tom jumped to his feet and ran for the back of the cabin. Something tripped him and he went sailing, hitting his face against the rear bulkhead.

"This is definitely boring," the Invisible Man said wearily. "How long will I have to bat you around this airship before you concede the inevitable and let me bop you over the head?"

"Go put some clothes on," Tom said.

"Do you think I actually like running about stark naked all the time? I'm quite fed up with it, if you must know the truth. But in my line of work, it's a necessity. Strangely enough, I've found that clothing is overrated. You don't need it half as much as you think you do. Of course, I do have to don a few things now and then, when the weather gets a bit too nippy."

Tom rued that canned spray paint hadn't been invented yet. There was nothing around for use as a substitute, either. Except . . . except maybe that cylinder strapped to the wall. A cylinder with a hose trailing out of it.

Tom got up and made another rough guess about the location of the voice, leaped, and missed again.

"Really, Olam, you're taking an awful drubbing, and I haven't laid a finger on you yet."

Tom slammed into the side of the fuselage again, this time directly under the cylinder. Striking like a snake, he reached for the thing, upended it, grabbed the hose, and sprayed in a wide pattern.

Tom grabbed a fire extinguisher and sprayed the compartment with white foam, and there he was:

Griffin—or his outline—in sodium bicarbonate. Tom threw the extinguisher at him and lunged.

It was tough wrestling with a semi-invisible man, but Tom got him in a full nelson and would not let go. Griffin kicked and stamped, but couldn't do much with bare feet. Tom maneuvered him to the side of the compartment and whomped his head into the bulkhead. Griffin went semi-limp, whereupon Tom whomped him again for good measure. The Invisible Man became the Unconscious Wet Noodle. Tom let him drop.

It was Tom's turn to be wrapped in a full nelson.

"Moriarty, give it up, for God's sake!"

"You've upset my plans once too often, Olam. I think I shall rid myself of you for good now."

Tom broke the hold using a classic wrestling countermove, whirled, and gut-punched Moriarty.

For the next half-minute or so, the two rolled around the airship, fighting, until it began to do strange things.

The bottom suddenly went out from under everything. Tom found himself floating free. The ship was diving. Apollo apparently had his own ideas.

Double cargo doors flew open. The ship banked steeply, and Tom and Moriarty slid toward the opening. Moriarty was holding onto Tom's trouser cuffs, dragging him to doom. Tom clawed at the smooth deck to no avail. Just then the craft banked the other way, doing a three-hundred-and-sixty-degree spin. The open hatch rotated, and Tom and Moriarty tumbled like clothes in a dryer. Both succeeded in rolling away from the open hatch when it became the floor. Moriarty, however, hit the ceiling heavily, and when the ship righted itself, he slumped to the deck, out cold.

As the fuselage continued to spin, something limp rolled over Tom. It was Griffin's body, presumably, with most of the calcite rubbed off. Tom lost sight of it and couldn't tell if it went out the hatch or not.

Loose objects were clattering all over the craft. One of them was the hammer, and Tom made a try at grabbing it. He missed, waited until the ship tilted the right way, leaped, and caught it. Thus armed, he made his way forward as the deck pitched this way and that, hanging on to a handy stanchion when Apollo tried another rollover.

Finally, he reached the pilot compartment, where he set to work smashing the hell out of the Zero Unit. He whacked at it a few times, then used the claw on it, trying to pry it out from its niche under the instrument panel. It didn't come out easily, and Tom had to resort to whacking it a few more times before it came loose, trailing a tangle of wires, linkages, and gears and shedding nuts and bolts by the dozen.

"How the hell did he get it installed so fast?" Tom said to no one in particular.

The ship began to drift. No one was guiding it now, its automatic pilot having been summarily ripped out. Tom threw the box on the floor and sat in the left seat. He grabbed the controls: two sticks, two pedals, and two throttle levers. The ship tilted left, and Tom pushed both sticks to the right. The ship corrected itself, then went over the other way.

OK, enough of this crap, he thought. When in doubt, reduce power.

He yanked both throttle levers; the engines died off, and the rotors slowed. But the ground began to come up a little too fast, so he pushed in both throttles slightly.

Something was crawling up his leg.

He yelped. It was the Zero Unit, its micro-armatures wrapping around his leg, clawing at him. He kicked at the thing, but it would not let go. He grabbed the hammer and whacked. The ground was coming up very fast now. He reached for the controls, but the thing had him by the arm now, and he felt metal teeth sink into his flesh. He screamed and bashed the metal monster wildly with the hammer, then whanged it against the back of the compartment, on the doorjamb, against the floor.

The ground was rushing up to meet him now. He made one last desperate attempt to pull out of the dive, wrenching back on the sticks, as the thing gnawed at his arm.

The ship hit the ground with a thud, bounced high, fell, and hit again. Then it slid into trees.

Tom found himself on the ceiling. Everything was quiet. He sat up and saw the box at his feet. Was it stunned? He looked around, found the hammer, got to his knees, and proceeded to smash the thing, over and over and over again, until he had reduced it to its various components. But even then it did not cease operations. Still left was a clutch of tiny, interlocking gears turning and turning. He smashed those, and when two or three of them fell away, he smashed the ones that still moved. He hit and hit again until he was sure nothing at all was moving. Then he sat and watched the resulting debris for any sign of activity. He thought he detected some slight twitching of a wire. He smashed it. A still-wobbling nut attracted his attention. He smashed that.

He got up and kicked the parts away, scattering them. Then he tossed the hammer aside.

He stumbled through the ship and out the still-open cargo doors. Moriarty was nowhere to be found. Neither was Griffin. They must have either fallen out or jumped. He didn't know, and didn't care.

He fell out of the wreckage, got to his feet, and turned to watch Mount Shasta explode.

Twenty-Three

"PEOPLE CAN MOVE quickly when they want to," Marianne said after sipping more of her wine. "I never saw so many people move so fast. They ran down that mountain."

She sat with Tom, Lady Ada, and Morrolan in one of Castle Falkenstein's many salons. Gilt tracery crawled up the pilasters and across the ceiling. On the walls hung colorful tapestries depicting unicorns cavorting in enchanted woods, maidens bathing in babbling streams, and other idyllic, classical scenes. Outside the Gothic windows, Castle Falkenstein's garden was in full midsummer bloom. A hint of jasmine came in on a warm breeze.

Lady Ada Lovelace sipped her tea. "We escaped by the skin of our teeth."

"Thank God the eruption was only a baby one," Marianne said.

"Morrolan, you couldn't have been in that lower chamber when the roof fell in," Ada said.

Morrolan set down his tea cup and saucer. "I was lucky not to be struck dead as soon as I altered that sand pentagram. I left the mountain immediately. Sorry I couldn't have warned you, but I was half expecting to be hit with a bolt of lightning at any time. I had to vacate immediately."

"Tom Olam," Marianne said, "you are being very impolite, reading that newspaper."

Tom set his paper down on the inlaid tea table. "Sorry. I can't believe they're still running stories about the Apollo conspiracy."

"What does the paper say?" Marianne asked.

"Oh, more articles about inactivated automatons showing up all over. People found supposedly dead, then the mortician gets a fright when he tries to embalm 'em."

"I think the most surprising development was that not all were duplicates," Ada said. "Apollo was cranking out automatons by the score, in factories all over the world. They assumed false identities, found employment, and took up their places in the world."

"One of the most fantastic plots ever," Morrolan said. "His magic was most efficacious, I must say. Admirable, in a way."

"Griffin's the admirable one," Tom said. "Such dedication to total madness is almost . . . well, I suppose it's almost like a religion with him."

"What about Moriarty?" Marianne said.

"His dedication to evil is satanic in the poetic sense," Ada said. "A true rebellion against the order of the universe. That's why he was drawn to Apollo. The two were alike. They would have inevitably fallen out, though. There is room for only one to reign in Hell."

"Tom, do you think Griffin is dead?" Marianne asked.

"We won't know unless he shows up somewhere."

"Strange thing to say about an invisible man," Ada commented.

"He'll show up," Tom said. "Anyway, he must have been in cahoots with Moriarty. Exactly when they linked is hard to say, but they did. And Griffin double-crossed his partner."

"It's a wonder criminal conspiracies are possible at all," Ada said. "They say there is honor among thieves, but I find it hard to believe."

"Anyway," Tom said, "that's the last convention of masterminds we'll see in a while. Good thing. I've had enough masterminds to last me for the rest of my life. In fact, I . . ."

Tom trailed off. Everybody watched agape as the teapot chose, of itself, to tip over and pour out a cup of tea. The teacup then floated upward.

"One thing about masterminds," came a voice whose source was unseen, "is that you never know what they're going to do next."

"Griffin!" Tom carefully set down his teacup.

"Hello. I hope you don't mind me dropping in like this. Fabulous castle, by the way. A trifle flamboyant, but impressive."

"Glad you like it. By the way, care to tell us what happened to Moriarty?"

"Oh, I saw him staggering away into the woods. I don't care what happened to him. I won't have anything to do with that blighter ever again. You can't trust him."

Tom glanced at Marianne. She was seated on the other side of the tea table, equidistant from the free-floating teacup. The look in her eyes gave him the cue.

They both dove for the teacup.

They succeeded only in cracking their heads together.

Griffin squealed in delight.

"Olam, I was going to repay you for that head-bashing you gave me, but I see you've done it to yourself. Again."

The laughter resounded through the high-ceilinged room, fading, fading.

Gone.

Tom held his aching head. "Who am I?"

"Oh, be quiet," Marianne said. "You're an idiot."

He grabbed her and they rolled over the parquetry like two kittens in mock combat.

Morrolan turned to Lady Ada. "They're such a nice couple."

In the grand tradition of Gibson and Sterling's Difference Engine and Tim Power's Anubis Gates comes a new steampunk epic.

FROM PRUSSIA WITH LOVE

A Castle Falkenstein™ Novel

John DeChancie

In the magical alternate Victorian universe of New Europa, good King Ludwig rules a mad empire of Faerie lords and ladies, spies, and scientists in a world where dragons, dwarfs and advanced steam technology are everyday reality. His stronghold is the mystical fortress born of this own fevered imagination and eldrich Faerie sorcery—Castle Falkenstein!

But when Ludwig's secret agents discover his archenemy, Chancellor Bismarck, is developing steam-powered intracontinental ballistic missiles, desperate measures are called for! Enter Tom Olam, 20th century computer game designer (and part-time secret agent), pulled by sorcery and subterfuge into New Europa to foil the Iron Chancellor's plot. His mission: infiltrate and sabotage the Prussian missile program, while King Ludwig, an Italian fireworks master, and the greatest dwarf engineer of all time struggle to create their own countermissile to save the Kingdom! Can they make it in time? Or does this spell the end of Castle Falkenstein?

John DeChancie is the author of numerous popular fantasy novels that remain perennially in print! His works include The Kruton Interface series, *Bride of the Castle, Castle Dreams, Castle Spellbound*, and co-authorship of *Dr. Dimension: Masters of Spacetime*.

ISBN 1-55958-772-4
U.S. $5.99
Canada $6.99
U.K. £4.99

Available now

THE LEAGUE OF DRAGONS

A Castle Falkenstein™ Novel

George Alec Effinger

Tom Olam and the lovely, swashbuckling Marianne meet Sherlock Holmes, the young, not-yet-famous hero of Sir Arthur Conan Doyle's series, on his first big adventure. Besides encountering Dr. Moriarty for the first time, Holmes must match wits with Dr. Fu Manchu. In the Castle Falkenstein universe, the Chinese supervillain isn't just an evil genius—he's a dragon! Fu Manchu has plans to use the Five Celestial Snows, Chinese herbal compounds of unthinkable power, to give China—and himself—control of the world. And only Holmes can stop him.

George Alec Effinger is a Hugo and Nebula award-winning author of more than 30 novels, including *When Gravity Fails* and *A Fire in the Sun*. In the early 1980s he wrote a novelization of the popular computer game *Zork!*

ISBN 0-7615-0243-2
U.S. $5.99
Canada $6.99
U.K. £4.99

Coming in October 1996

CHRONOMASTER

A Novel by Jane Lindskold

SYNOPSIS: At least two pocket universes are in mysterious states: no one can get in or out. All trade is stalled, and no one knows what happened, or what to do about it.

No one doubts Rene Korda is the best man for the job, except Rene Korda. He's retired. He likes sitting back on his ship and listening to the rain. He doesn't want to go traipsing around pocket universes where the laws of physics work in different ways, saving the world for mega-business.

But his ship's computer is an impudent personality Korda names Jester, and she won't leave him alone until he at least talks to the recruiter. And he wouldn't be the best man for the job if he couldn't be intrigued by a problem. But this time, even Korda may have bitten off more than he can chew.

Jane Lindskold is the author of *Brother to Dragons, Companion to Owls, Marks of Our Brothers, Nine Princes in Amber, Trumps of Doom,* and other novels. Before he died, Roger Zelany described her as "terrific . . . one of the brightest new writers to come along in years."

Roger Zelany is a household word in science fiction and fantasy. He is the award-winning and best-selling author of the *Amber* series.

ISBN: 0-7615-0422-2 PRICE: $5.99 U.S./$6.99 Can./£4.99 U.K.

COMING IN MAY 1996

QuantumGate

A Novel by Jane E. Hawkins

SYNOPSIS: Drew Griffin, astronaut, is charged with defying the threat to the planet Earth. To reach this goal, he must go to distant planet AJ3905, and obtain the rare iridium oxide, humanity's only chance of reversing the coming environmental Armageddon. But the denizens of AJ3905 don't necessarily care about Earth, and they're not there to make Griffin's task a simple one!

Jane E. Hawkins is a mathematician and computer programmer who lives in Seattle, Washington.

> "Better than any since Blade Runner...
> a future shock film on par with Aliens."
> —Computer Gaming World on Hyperbole's
> Quantum Gate

ISBN: 0-7615-0198-3   PRICE: $5.99 U.S./$6.99 Can./£4.99 U.K.

COMING IN APRIL 1996

**Are they thieves from the future,
or rescuers of irreplaceable artifacts?**

OBELISK

A Novel by Judith Jones

SYNOPSIS: In the present Egyptologist Virginia Alexander is assigned to investigate the mysterious disappearance of artifacts from Egyptology collections around the world.

In the future archaeologist and historian John Howard is stymied in his work by the huge amount of historial material that was lost in the Cataclysm of 2479. When an alien technology makes time travel possible, Howard becomes obsessed with retrieving an unimaginable hoard of artifacts: the treasure trove of humanity's history.

Judith Jones is a professional Egyptologist and the author of Obelisk, the computer game. She lives in Fremont, California.

ISBN: 0-7615-0419-2   PRICE: $5.99 U.S./$6.99 Can./£4.99 U.K.

COMING IN FALL 1996

Other Proteus Books Now Available from Prima!

Hardcover

In The 1st Degree: A Novel $19.95
Dominic Stone

The 7th Guest: A Novel $21.95
Matthew J. Costello and Craig Gardner

Paperback

From Prussia with Love: $5.99
       A Castle Falkenstein Novel
John DeChancie

Hell: A Cyberpunk Thriller—A Novel $5.99
Chet Williamson

The Pandora Directive: A Tex Murphy Novel $5.99
Aaron Conners

Star Crusader: A Novel $5.99
Bruce Balfour

Wizardry: The League of the $5.99
       Crimson Crescent—A Novel
James Reagan

X-COM UFO Defense: A Novel $5.99
Diane Duane

FILL IN AND MAIL TODAY

PRIMA PUBLISHING
P.O. BOX 1260BK
ROCKLIN, CA 95677

USE YOUR VISA/MC AND ORDER BY PHONE:
(916) 632-4400 (M-F 9:00-4:00 PST)

Please send me the following titles:

Quantity	Title	Amount

Subtotal $_____

Postage & Handling
($4.00 for the first book
plus $1.00 each additional book) $ _____

Sales Tax
7.25% Sales Tax (California only)
8.25% Sales Tax (Tennessee only)
5.00% Sales Tax (Maryland only)
7.00% General Service Tax (Canada) $_____

TOTAL *(U.S. funds only)* $_____

Check enclosed for $_____(payable to Prima Publishing)
Charge my   Master Card   Visa

Account No. _____Exp. Date _____

Signature _____

Your Name _____

Address _____

City/State/Zip _____

Daytime Telephone _____

Satisfaction is guaranteed— or your money back!
Please allow three to four weeks for delivery.
THANK YOU FOR YOUR ORDER